Also by Teresa Collard

Published by Severn House Ltd:
Murder at the Tower
Murder at the Royal Shakespeare Theatre
Murder at Hampton Court Palace

Published by First Century
The Sun Should Never Shine
But for the Grace of God

After leaving RADA, Teresa Collard has spent her life involved in the Arts. She was the first administrator at the Swan Theatre, Worcester then on to Questers Theatre, Ealing. She was the first manager at the Neptune theatre, Liverpool, where she established the Neptune Theatre Company and ran art exhibitions. It was there that a love for children's entertainment developed. She wrote and directed children's plays and documentaries before going on to run the Bluecoat Art Gallery in Liverpool. After Liverpool she became Arts and Entertainment Manager for the Borough of Milton Keynes. A notable achievement was the highly acclaimed February Festival (1977 – 1983). Together with the composer David Lyon she developed performances for children based on history, in which the audience were totally involved, starting with the nationally acclaimed Battle of Trafalgar. Later they produced Charter Extravaganza, based on the history of Northamptonshire, which was performed in Northampton and at The Albert Hall. In the 1980s she moved to the village of Hanwell in Oxfordshire, where she began writing murder mysteries.

Operation Giselle © Teresa Collard

ISBN 978-1-291-39229-6

Copyright © Teresa Collard 2012

OPERATION GISELLE
Previously published as 'The Sun Should Never Shine'

Teresa Collard

Dedicated to Bomber Command

In 2004 I dedicated this book, published under the title 'The Sun Should Never Shine', to Bomber Command, who at that time, had not been awarded medals for their courage and extraordinary bravery. Since then, thank the Lord, they have been awarded the medals that they deserve and in March 2012 a memorial for their bravery was placed in London's Green Park.

ONE

1989

Six weeks. "Six weeks," the Assistant Chief Constable had said, "and don't let me see you materialise until July the first.'

Inspector Julian Venning knew exactly how he'd like to spend the next six weeks. Thought about it as he drove back to his cottage on the green at Yarnton. In all his fifteen years since passing out at Police College he'd never managed more that fourteen days leave. The ACC was right. Of course, he was fagged out. It had been a particularly gruelling case, working round the clock for months on end, but finally they'd cornered the bastard, the provider, the smart looking businessman dealing in imports and exports with an office in the heart of Oxford. More imports than exports. Drugs were not the Inspector's field. He'd been seconded to the Drug Squad because he knew his way around the colleges and halls of residence. Knew the dives where commodity and money changed hands.

A policeman, 6' 2", broad, red headed, and red bearded was hardly an invisible aid, but somehow he'd managed to merge. Disgusting jeans, rumpled shirt, unkempt beard, and greasy hair had made him look like the archetypal middle aged hippy.

The dealer, thank God, had been sent down for ten years. Not enough in the Inspector's view, not nearly enough for the misery he'd caused. It would have been more but for the brilliant Defence Counsel who'd succeeded in making a hardened police inspector feel that he, not the dealer, was on trial. Venning decided whilst the Jury was deliberating that he'd take Joyce and Judith to Scotland. It was a country he scarcely knew. Why not meander round the Highlands, see Lochness, the Cairngorms, Glencoe and over the sea to Skye? Go where the road led them. He'd float the idea, see how Joyce re-acted, but there, he thought ruefully, was the rub. Would she as things stood be willing to go on holiday? The irony was that they could do nothing by staying at home. The answerphone would record any messages, easy enough to pick up whether they were in Scotland, or Timbuctoo. But it was not to be.

> 'A holiday, Julian! You must be joking. Father has been missing for nearly a month..
> Why the hell did he have to do this to us? He's all but seventy he should have had more sense.'

Venning looked into his wife's tired blue eyes with compassion, read the misery, noticed too that she'd not bothered with her make-up, nor had she coiled her long luscious hair round her head. He knew that every time Joyce thought about her father she also thought about her daughter Susan, still blaming herself for a needless accident. After a bitter argument her first husband Keith grabbed Susan who, much to her mother's fury, had not finished her homework. He shoved the child into the passenger seat of his Mercedes and in a flaming temper drove recklessly down the M40. ..By the time he arrived a scene of utter carnage both father and child had been pronounced dead. From the beginning of the enquiry he'd done everything possible to protect and comfort Joyce, more than a policeman should have, but he'd recognised a replay of his own marriage. Sometimes he wondered if he hadn't found divorce more traumatic than an accident. .

'What are you thinking about, Jules? Why don't you say something? What do you really think has happened to Dad?'

'I don't know any more than you do.'

'You haven't really looked for him, have you?'

'I can't push it too hard, Joyce, because technically he is not a missing person. He told the Fletchers he'd be away for a couple of weeks and asked them to look after Napoleon. He obviously means to return.'

'But, Jules, it's nearly four weeks. Anything could have happened.'

'Yes, my love, but I can't help feeling Andrew knows exactly what he's doing. At this moment he's probably sitting in the Opera House in Rome lapping up a performance of *Aida*.'

'But that's not what you said yesterday.'

'Can't you see, Joyce, I'm guessing. We must chat up the neighbours, they may have heard from him because we don't know whether he's in this country or abroad. We don't know whether he travelled by bus, train, boat or plane. All we know is, that he's not driving his own car.' He had to say what he was thinking, hurtful or not. 'He does not want to be found, Joyce. That's why he left his car in the garage. A car is the easiest thing in the world to trace. Your father, needed to escape, get rid of all the aggro and stress of the past few years. Remember he was forced into early retirement when your mother, against doctor's orders, took to her bed. A demanding lady your mother., you said so yourself, now he needs to find peace, come to terms with a whole new life in which he can do exactly as he pleases. No more washing, ironing, cooking, cleaning, shopping, or nursing. He's free! Doesn't want to be found. You must face facts, darling, your mother was exhausting, and for some reason, best known to herself, she needed your father at her beck and call.'

'Everything you say about mother is true, but you're wrong about father. He's not out there searching for peace, because despite mother's demands, he always found inner strength in his beloved garden.' She smiled to herself when she thought of him looking like an aged hippy wandering round the garden with a Walkman strung round his neck, talking to the plants, or explaining to Napoleon that cats who never listen to opera miss one of the greatest wonders of the world. Tears coursed down her face. She mustn't cry, she'd cried enough.

'Sorry, darling, I didn't mean you to come home to this. The whole business has got on top of me. Anyway, you haven't told me why you're home so early.'

'It's all over.'

'What!'

'The jury, God bless 'em, was out for less than an hour, and to a man they found that nauseating drug dealer guilty. He's gone down for ten years.'

'I thought you said that there were two women on the jury.'

He laughed. 'Yes, you're right. A figure of speech.'

'You'll never learn, will you! Anyway I'm glad it's all over, now, perhaps, you can get some rest.'

'We have six weeks, darling,' he said quietly, 'six weeks to do what we like, go where we like, Scotland, Wales or even where we could enjoy continental cuisine..'

'But, Jules, I can't, not while..........'

'I know,' he sighed.

'And there's another thing......'

'Yes?'

'Napoleon. We can't leave the Fletchers feeding him for ever. We'll have to do something about it.'

'Like what?.'

'Perhaps we should go over to Northampton tomorrow, have a word with Mrs Fletcher and if she finds it inconvenient, take Napoleon to a cattery?'

Venning exploded. 'Joyce don't you realise I am on leave. I hadn't planned on driving backwards and forwards to Northampton to deal with Siamese cats.'

'One cat, and he's a Siamese crossed with a Blue Persian.'

'I don't care whether he's crossed with a bloody tiger, I don't care what he is---let the people next door get on with doing what they've been doing. I thought the Fletchers loved cats?'

'So they do, but they may be going on holiday. Tell you what, Julian, I'll go over in the morning, with Judith. We'll take a sandwich lunch. You have a lie-in.'

He caved in. 'Okay, okay, I'll come with you, and while I'm in Northampton I'll call at the station, see Chief Inspector Browne, put him in the picture about your father, give him our car number in case we decide to go on holiday and something untoward develops. We'll keep our options open.'

'Let me think about it.' Her expression said it all.

Saturday morning traffic on the A43 from Oxford to Northampton was a go-slow exercise. Judith talked non-stop all the way, or so it seemed to her father who had plenty to think about. He merely grunted in reply, which could be taken as either 'yes' or 'no'.

'Why can't we take Napoleon home with us, Mummy?'

'We could, I suppose, if the Fletchers have had enough.'

Operation Giselle © Teresa Collard   5

Venning, for once, managed more than a grunt. 'Oh no, we don't. We have enough problems without a Corsican general on our hands who might suddenly take it into his head to become an emperor.'

'What do you mean, Daddy?'

'I mean that we're not having Napoleon to stay. We'd be tied to the house.' He didn't elaborate, didn't explain what was going on in his Machiavellian mind.

It was nearly noon before they let themselves into Andrew Pringle's semi-detached house in Venning Hill which he'd named *Cartref*.

'What does *Cartref* mean, Mummy?'

'Home, in Welsh. My grandmother was Welsh, my father likes to remember that.'

'Why aren't you Welsh then?'

'Because my father was born in England, here in Northampton.'

'I'd like to be Welsh and wear one of those funny hats,' said Judith wistfully.

The door mat was covered in free papers, two letters, an electricity bill, and brochures advertising everything from double-glazing to a DIY swimming pool. The house smelt musty, full of warm stale air and a strong smell one associates with cats. Joyce flung open all the windows and patio doors. The lawn, once so lovingly attended, badly needed cutting, and weeds were rampant. Judith, who had heard the children next door, ran into the garden and climbed over the fence.

'She'll be happy, Jules for the next hour, so let's glance at the mail.'

'You really are something else, Joyce. A perfect mother for my child. More than I deserve.'

'It was meant to be,' she whispered. 'Judith last saw her mother when she was three, never mentions her, so I often wonder whether she even remembers her. Judith and Susan would have been perfect playmates.'

'Come on, Joyce, sit on the patio while I find the booze. The mail can wait.'

'Julian, he's not coming back, is he?'

'I have no idea.'

'He wouldn't leave the garden for so long, not at this time of the year with the roses in full bloom, and the hydrangeas at their best.'

As Venning returned to the house he came to a rapid decision. He was going to have a holiday, come what may, even if it turned out to be a busman's holiday. He found a bottle of whisky, soda and two glasses and took them out on to the patio.

'Do sit down, Joyce, relax, and listen to what I have to say.'

'Not if we're going to discuss holidays.'

'We are, but a holiday with a difference.'

Reluctantly she took the proffered whisky and sat down on a bench..

'I have six weeks freedom, the longest vacation I'm ever likely to have, so let's make the most of it, use the time to find your father?'

'Julian, you can't do that, you should rest, besides I'd feel guilty....'

'That's nonsense. There's no need to feel guilty. I'll not be able to put my feet up while you're in such a state. We'll join forces, and look for your old man?'

'What good will I be?'

'You have everything in your head. Sit back and dredge up every memory you have of your father. We'll stay here for a couple of days.........'

'But we've no night clothes, not even a tooth brush.'

'I'm sure you can find something of your mother's.'

'Oh no, I couldn't do that.'

'Why ever not?'

'She's dead, Jules. It would give me the creeps to wear her clothes. I'll buy what we need.'

'Okay, but don't waste money on pyjamas for me. I can manage without.'

'Let's go home, I can't see the point of spending two days here.'

'We need time, Joyce, to go through every cupboard, every drawer, look through photograph albums, and letters. Something may point us in the right direction. Also you must have an in depth discussion with Mavis next door.'

She shook her head.

Venning knew his wife had a right to be worried. The state of the garden said it all.

'Joyce you must talk to the Fletchers, find out if your father gave the faintest hint about his movements, and on Monday I'll talk to his ex-colleagues at the Municipal Offices. We have to face the problem squarely. Find out what has driven him away, and be prepared for the worst.

'What do you mean by the worst?'

'I don't know, darling, because I hardly knew your father. Are you going to help me?'

'Of course I am. But what are we going to tell Judith?'

'The truth.'

Joyce smiled at her husband, the first time he'd seen such a smile for weeks. 'You're something else, my darling, you really are.'

She jumped up, dashed into the hall and from a vast pile of junk mail she retrieved two letters. 'Open them, Julian, ' she said handing them to him.

He slit open the first with his penknife, and glanced at a typewritten letter inviting Andrew Pringle to rejoin the Weston Favell Tennis Club.

'How long since your father played?'

'About four years, until things became too traumatic like Mum constantly ringing the club and asking him to come back home on some pretext or other. What's the other letter about?'

'Interesting! No stamp. Delivered by hand. All it says is *Andrew, Do you need the books you left behind with my brother Francis? He's been ringing you, but answer came there none? Colin Dadswell.*

'Let's see.' Joyce took the letter. 'There's no address.'

'Not difficult to trace, my darling. There can't be many Dadswells in the Northampton telephone directory, go and do a bit of research.'

Joyce was up before he'd finished speaking. He laughed out loud. Even if he wasn't looking forward to a busman's holiday his wife was going to enjoy it.

'Eureka,' she shouted. 'we're in luck, darling. There are only two, an *A Dadswell*, and a *C Dadswell,* in Church Lane, Weston Favell. That's ever so close, less than a mile away.'

'Excellent. You'd better call him.'

'What am I going to say?'

'Ask him if I could pop round this afternoon for a short chat about your father, and while you're doing that I'll sink another whisky before mowing the lawn. After that I could browse through the photograph albums that are in the sitting room bookcase.'

The lawn mower gave a cough, spluttered and finally gave up the ghost. The machine had run out of its life blood. Damn, thought Venning, now it will have to wait. He wiped the sweat off his brow, and had a quick wash before settling down on the patio to leaf through three albums. Joyce with her parents at two years, then at five years holding her father's hand by the lake in Abington Park. Snapshots of Joyce were plentiful until she reached the age of nineteen when she left home to become an assistant matron in a boarding school. The third album was devoted to holiday scenes of more recent years. Andrew and Emily at Rhyl, Eastbourne, Bath, St Ives then latterly in France, but always with the car. The last photographs, taken three years ago, showed the invalid sitting in her wheel chair at the bottom of stone steps outside a small church. Several people had emerged from the church all looking distressed, some with handkerchiefs to their faces, others wiping their eyes with the back of their hands. How odd to take pictures of strangers attending a funeral service. The next four pictures were even more peculiar; a Singer sewing machine standing outside a derelict house; a ruined schoolhouse; a burnt out pre-war Renault; broken overhead lines for a trolley bus that could never possibly arrive. A ruined village. Why, he wondered, had it been abandoned? He turned the page to find a black and white photograph of Emily Pringle staring straight at him from the comfort of a wheelchair. She was a big lady, must have taken quite a deal of muscle to push her around the village. In one snapshot a long shadow fell between the chair and the photographer who was obviously Andrew. In another a monumental cenotaph with several hundred names inscribed upon its walls towered above a grave yard. Must have been a battle on the site of this village, but what on earth possessed Andrew, why so many depressing pictures?

Joyce disturbed his reverie by leaning out of the back bedroom window shouting excitedly that she'd found a box of letters, a file of newspaper cuttings, a sealed envelope, and another photograph album.

'Shall we go through them now?'

'No, keep hunting, see if you can find anything else and we'll take a look at them tonight.'

'Why haven't you finished the lawn?'

'Ran out of juice. Did you manage to raise Colin Dadswell?'

'Yeah. Okay fro this afternoon.'

'Good, and darling make sure you get some petrol fro the mower while you're shopping this afternoon, but let's eat now because I'm, ravenous.'

Judith rushed in, collected her sandwiches, and rushed out again to join the children next door for a picnic at the end of their garden. Her absence gave her father time during a leisurely lunch, his senses assailed by the smell of newly cut grass, to learn something of his father-in-law's background.

Andrew, it seems, during the poverty stricken late 30s had worked as a clerk in a shoe factory, but in August 1939, before war was declared, he'd joined the Royal Air Force. Being bright he became a pilot but only as Joyce retold the family history did she realise how little she knew about her father. He'd hardly ever mentioned the war. In fact if the subject cropped up he pointedly left the room, or if there was a mention on radio or TV he turned it off.

'It was weird,' said Joyce, 'when you think about it, because it was the one and only subject where Mum had no say. She neither remonstrated nor interfered. If he wanted the television turned off, it was turned off. Not only that he never bought or wore a poppy on Remembrance Day. Odd, don't you think, for someone who fought from the beginning to the end of the war not to be interested?'

'I agree with you. Makes one wonder what caused the hang-up? Perhaps he felt like Siegfried Sassoon, who after being awarded the M.C. decided pacifism was the only sane course.'

'I am positive he wasn't a pacifist. Underneath his sort of laid-back approach to life there was a hard unforgivable streak, yet as a father he was the kindest man imaginable.'

'Did he keep a diary?'

'I don't know, but the past five years would have made boring reading. Who wants to write about washing, ironing, shopping and housework?'

'It will have to be black coffee, darling. There's no milk until I've been shopping.'

'No problem. It'll keep my weight down.'

Standing in the kitchen in her bare feet, Joyce thought how little it had changed since her childhood. The same crockery, the same furniture, the same oven; only the curtains were different. Suddenly she heard her parents arguing as she'd heard them when she was nine years old. On a hot stifling night she'd crept down to the kitchen for a drink of water. All the doors were open. Her father was speaking to her mother in the sitting room in a voice she'd never heard before, a cold dispassionate voice, then her mother's softer tones almost pleading with him.

"*Vengeance, he said in a steely inhuman way, ' is what I shall have..*"

"*Don't talk like that, Andrew. Isn't it about time you learnt to live with it? Thousands of people have, so why should it be any different for you?*"

"*It was cold-blooded murder. Do you think I should stand by and do nothing, absolutely nothing when……………….*"

She missed the rest because her father walked out on to the patio, but her mother's raised voice carried, each word clearly audible.

"*It was seventeen years ago, and let's face it, you've neither the time nor the money for a vendetta.*" Joyce remembered wondering what a vendetta was, but her mother wouldn't let go.

"*Andrew, you've allowed this memory to destroy you. You've no room in your heart any more for a normal family relationship. No love there at all. All you can think about is the past. If only you could pour your energy and hate into creating a garden, taking an interest in what Joyce does, and attending chapel with me, then I think you might find a little happiness.*"

Until that moment Joyce had never thought of her mother as suffering. Had she realised that then the relationship between them could have been so different. Her father, to some extent, had taken her mother's advice. He had created a wonderful garden; he had taken her out and about, to the park, the swings, to the circus and pantomimes, but never attended chapel. She had to go with her mother, and how she hated it, but why hadn't she understood? The conversation, she remembered, had frightened her, she'd scampered upstairs without having a drink, and buried her head under the bedclothes.

TWO

Colin Dadswell was in his garden weeding when the inspector arrived. From under the brim of a battered hat he smiled at the intruder. 'Good afternoon! Inspector Venning, isn't it?'

'Yes. Thanks for agreeing to see me at such short notice.'

'It's nothing. Can't shake hands, old man, they're too grubby. Go round the back, find yourself a pew, while I have a quick wash, then you can tell me what's cooking.'

Venning parked himself on a garden bench in front of a massive bank of blue hydrangeas effectively masking the kitchen garden. Twenty four hours ago, he thought, I was in court never dreaming I'd be straight into the throes of another case, the case of my missing father-in-law. Sounds like a Conan Doyle short story, but there's no way it will be short, too much like the proverbial needle. We'll be lucky to find Andrew, who manifestly doesn't want to be found.

His host emerged from the backdoor carrying two mugs of tea and a sugar basin. 'Hope you take milk, Mr Venning, because I've already put it in.'

'Yes, I do.'

'My wife's shopping which gives us plenty of time to discuss Andrew. If she were here I'd not get a word in edgeways.'

'You knew Andrew well, did you?'

'No, not really. No one knew him well. Some days he'd go for hours without communicating, yet on his day he could be amusing and charming, though my wife, if she were here, would tell you he had too many off days.'

'You worked together, did you?'

'Yes, we were both in the Borough Legal Department. Andrew was in charge of the library and filing systems, which by the time he left were all on computer.'

'How is it that he knew your brother?'

'He didn't, but for some reason, which he never explained, he desperately wanted to visit Berlin, possibly for the opera, that would be my guess. He asked for an intro to my brother who's a Group Captain, in fact he's the Senior Officer in Berlin. Francis, or Frank as we call him, is also an opera buff so they'll have a lot to talk about when they eventually meet up.'

'Why exactly are you here, Mr Venning? Andrew could have told you all this.'

'Andrew is missing.'

'What! Since when?'

'Nearly four weeks now, only two months after the desath of my mother-in-law.

'Doesn't really surprise me. Off to fresh fields and pastures new, which is precisely what he needed, so why try to find him?'

'Joyce, my wife, is worried. She thinks her father's gone for good, and the only clue we have is your note about his books.'

'But he could be anywhere, the world's now his oyster, although, come to think about it, Germany makes sense because he's so keen on everything Germanic, that's why he has studied the language for years.'

'Good God! Why on earth didn't my wife mention that?'

'She may not have known. He went to night classes for a brief spell some six or seven years ago but found them pretty useless. I heard that after he'd retired he booked a day-course run by Ed Watkins at the college of further education. Oh, yes, nearly forgot. While still working he bought one of those language courses on tape which helped him quite a bit. In fact when Germans visited the Municipal Offices he was able to converse, albeit slowly. Read a lot of books too, always in his lunch hour, never wasted a minute.'

'What sort of books?'

'All to do with Germany. Fodor's Germany, the Blue Guide to Berlin, Modern Berlin, Berlin Divided, to name but a few. He must know Berlin like the back of his hand.'

'Your brother's on the phone, presumably?'

'Oh yes, but it's ex-directory. All this security business, but you'll be able to contact him at the office.'

'He doesn't live at HQ then?'

'Yes, he has a grace and favour residence. Five bedrooms for two of them in a sumptious house fit for an ambassador. Mollycoddled, you know, because it's a quasi-diplomatic job. We were in the wrong business, Andrew and I. No perks in local government. And yet Angela does nothing but complain.'

'Angela?'

'My brother's wife. I have never discovered why she married into the service. Every one knows it's normally two years here, and two years there. Here today and gone tomorrow, you might say.'

'How long has your brother been in Berlin?'

'He hit gold this time. Did two years in the fifties, soon after the wall went up, then several years in the States before returning to Berlin in 85. He's likely to finish his career there, which will suit him. Mad on Wagner, you know.'

'Have you been to Berlin, Mr Dadswell?'

'Yes, but once was enough. Nice enough place, plenty to do, but Angela gets up my nose.'

Venning left the disgruntled local government officer and walked up Churchway, past the Trumpet Inn and into the main road thinking about his father-in-law, a stranger whom he'd first met four years ago at their Registry Office wedding in Oxford. Knowing Andrew a little better might have helped to prevent all this. A pity there'd not been enough time, but that was the story of his life.

As he opened the front door he heard Judith's high pitched squeal of delight accompanied by the sound which only a Siamese can produce.

Joyce shouted down the stairs. 'Take him into the garden, Judith. Let him play in the long grass where he can pretend to be a tiger.'

The sounds of both child and cat grew fainter, and Joyce came down the stairs struggling with a case she'd filled with her father's papers.

'Here give it me.' He carried it downstairs and into the front room. 'Gosh it's heavy.'

'Of course it's heavy, there's an awful lot of reading there. It's full of letters, newspaper cuttings, notes and diaries, and Julian I don't think...' She stopped.

'What don't you think?'

'I've mixed feelings about doing this. It seemed such a good idea ... I do want to find him, but we'll be prying ... You do this sort of thing every day of the week, it doesn't mean anything to you.'

'Oh yes it does, but we've no option, there's nothing else to go on.'

'Yes, there is. I've just been round to the Fletchers to ask them if they'd heard from Dad. They were a bit cagey, gave me the feeling that they're not sure whether he's coming back. I'm frightened, Julian.'

'There's no need to be. I promise you we'll find him.'

'He gave them a £100 before he left to cover the cost of Napoleon's food and a stay at Moulton Cattery if and when they go on holiday. He's definitely gone abroad.. Ron told me that Dad didn't want to be driven to Heathrow but Ron insisted. On the way Dad told him that he was catching a plane to Rome because he wanted to see *Rigoletto* performed in the Baths of Caracalla. Darling, he's thought of everything, but at least he's alive because he rang three days ago to find out whether Napoleon was fit and whether we'd contacted them. Mavis told him everything was okay, and not to worry because they'd mow the lawn.'

'They were a bit slow on the draw,' said Venning feelingly.

'They intended doing it tomorrow.'

'Do they know where he phoned from?'

'No. Mrs Fletcher took the call, said he sounded so clear he could have been in the next room.'

'You know something,' said Joyce suddenly, 'we haven't looked in the loft'

'Oh Lord, never gave it a thought.'

It was easy enough to switch on the loft light, open the trap door, and let down the ladder, but the aperture was small and Venning was large. He gradually eased himself through the hole and sat with his legs dangling while he took stock of what was up in the roof space. There was, in fact, very little, not surprising because the trap was too small for large suitcases and boxes. By stretching he was able to reach two shoe boxes, and an old fashioned metal brief case. He opened one of the boxes to find a motley selection of horse brasses and in the other a dozen bone-handled knives. He replaced them before trying to open the metal case. It was locked. 'Joyce,' he yelled, have you come across any keys in your search?'

'Yes, I saw three or four in the top drawer of the dressing table.'

'Good girl, I'll bring this brief case down and see what we can do.'

As he closed the trap door it came to him in a flash that Colin Dadswell had been less than helpful over his brother's phone number. He must have given it to Andrew. Anyone of such an exalted rank reaching the end of his service life would probably be spending more time at home than in his office. A sinecure of a job. He wanted that number like NOW. Detective Sergeant Paxton was his best bet. He'd call him and ask him to tap into Charlie who would, of course, spew out the ex-directory number without any argument.

Paxton, on a long weekend duty was sitting at DHQ twiddling his thumbs. Any diversion was welcome.

'Yes, sir, if you'd care to hang on, I'll get Charlie motivated.'

Venning could hear him tapping away at the keys and talking to himself. 'Got it,' he shouted. 'Hello, sir. Group Captain Dadswell can be reached on 010 49 30 0909.'

'Thanks Keith. Give Charlie a pat on the back, he's done it again.'

'If there's anything else you need, sir, let me know, but half a mo aren't you supposed to be on holiday?'

'Yes Keith, a busman's holiday.' Paxton laughed as he replaced the receiver.

The number rang out only three times before it was answered by a woman who sounded unutterably bored.

'Angela Dadswell,' she said using the squashed vowel sounds of those who like to think they're upper class. Crawss instead of cross, and in Angela's case, Dedswell instead of Dadswell.'

'Detective Inspector Venning here, madam. May I speak to your husband?'

'Is it anything serious? You can tell me.'

'No, madam, not serious, but I would like a few words with your husband.'

'Very well,' she said. patently annoyed, 'I will fetch him.'

'Dadswell here.'

'Good morning, sir. I understand from your brother Colin Dadswell, whom I met this afternoon, that you may have had contact with Andrew Pringle.'

'I may have had.'

A cold response. Why wondered the Inspector. 'It's imperative, sir, that I get in touch with him immediately.'

'You are a policeman, so perhaps you'd better tell me what's going on? What's he wanted for?'

'He's not wanted for anything, sir. He is missing and I need to trace his whereabouts.'

'Missing, is he! That's not a crime is it, Inspector?'

'No, sir.'

'I believe in this free and democratic society of ours we should be able to go where we like, when we like, without anyone asking questions.'

The Inspector was justifiably annoyed. 'Do you usually block police enquiries, sir, or is it that you've been too close to events in Eastern Europe for so long that you prize freedom above all else? What about safety,? And what about family affiliations? His daughter has asked for my help.'

'That doesn't make an iota of difference, Inspector. If Mr Pringle wants to contact his daughter, all he has to do is pick up a phone, which means he must have a perfectly valid reason for not wanting to be found.'

'If you see him,' said Venning attempting to control his impatience, 'will you please ask him to get in touch immediately.'

'If Mr Pringle cares to visit me I will pass on your message. Good day, sir.'

Julian Venning swore softly to himself. His sixth sense told him that Andrew had already met Dadswell but not to discuss the merits of opera. Damn! Their quarry could be anywhere, but there was nothing more they could do until Andrew's papers and diaries had been sifted and read.

As soon as Judith was tucked up in bed with her teddy they settled down at the dining room table to examine the contents of one of the cases. While Joyce extracted the diaries Venning tried numerous keys in an attempt to open the metal box, but it didn't budge and its secrets remained intact. The diaries covering 1950-1970 told them nothing. All they contained were details of office appointments, times of tennis matches and a few notes about operas that Andrew had attended. There was a reference to a Sunday concert held in a church in Newport Pagnell. *This young bass, John Tomlinson will go far. One day he'll be classed with Boris Christoff, and Chaliapin. His singing in Rossini's Petit Messe Solonelle was both moving and memorable.*

Joyce laughed when she found stories she'd written in 1968. 'I was only eight when these were written. Fancy keeping them!'

'Perhaps he thought you'd be a second Catherine Cookson.'

'I doubt it.' Despite the warm night Joyce shivered slightly. 'It's a funny feeling I have, Julian, about all this. Almost as if my father's secret world was here in these papers, as though he picked them up from time to time to relive the past.'

'I am sure he did. You have only to look at the newspaper cuttings to see how often they've been handled.'

'But it doesn't make any sense. He never ever talked about the war, but he thought about it, didn't he, because every one of these cuttings is either about the RAF or the Luftwaffe?

'Yes, you're right.' He yawned, they were going to have another late night. 'Let's take a cursory glance at the contents of the other case before I have another shot at opening the metal box.'

'Coffee, I think,' said Joyce. We need something to keep us awake.'

Two hours later after coffees, improved with generous helping of brandy, they had read dozens of letters, newspaper cuttings and three five-year diaries covering 1971-1985.

'Julian, why should they finish in 1985? What's happened in 1986 through to 1990?

Joyce watched as her husband picked up the last diary and thumbed through it.

'You're right ? It finishes on June 9th, 1985. After that, nothing. They were on holiday. Just look at this.

June 6 *Portsmouth to Le Havre. Arrive 7 a.m.*
June 7 *Bernay. Du Lion D'or,*
June 8 *Chartres. Du Boueuf Couronne. Visit Cathedral*
June 9 *Montlucon. Le Fiacre*
June 10 *Limoges. Lion D'or. Visit Oradour-s-Glane*
And there it stops.'

'That was their last holiday. Dad pushed Mum around in the wheelchair. He came back on his knees.'

'How long were they away?'

'Nearly three weeks, I think.'

'So what did they do after June 10th? That was the night they spent at Limoges, and why has nothing been recorded?'

'You tell me.'

By midnight they were too tired to concentrate any more and were about to go to bed when Juliang remembered he hadn't opened the metal box. Joyce was apprehensive.

'Do you think we ought to open it? It could be like Pandora's box full of unexpected ills and misery.'

'If we're to find Andrew we need to know everything about him, especially his hang-ups which may lead us to the motivation for his vanishing trick. We have to delve into his past.'

'All right, I suppose you must.'

He found a stout screwdriver and pressed it under the hasp and with one quick jerk broke open the lock. Carefully he removed the contents and placed them on the kitchen table. Joyce picked up the only newspaper cutting.

'This is quite recent. *The Times, Saturday April 25 1987* headed *German veterans relive secret operation.* They both gazed at a photograph of nine ex-Junkers pilots posing in the RAF Museum at Hendon.

'What on earth did he want this for. Just read that third paragraph, Julian.'

In March 1945, only weeks before the end of the war, the Luftwaffe launched, Operation Giselle, a plan designed to destroy RAF bombers as they came into land at their home bases.

'Why isn't this cutting with all the other clippings?'

'You tell me, Julian, you're the detective. Hi,! she yelled, 'just look at this. It's a book on Oradour. Gancing at the first page he recognised a familiar image. A cenotaph in a village cemetery. The last photograph in Andrew's holiday album.

'And here are his birth certificates. Why on earth did he need two?' She opened them out.

'Peter John Pringle, born December 15th 1921. Good Lord, why did he change his name?' She looked at the other certificate in total disbelief.

'Andrew Paul Pringle, born December 15th 1921. I don't believe it, Julian.'

He took the certificates out of her hand. 'Peter and Andrew December 15th 1921. They were twins, Joyce. Your father had a brother.'

Joyce wandered round the room, dazed. She talked to her father as if he were in the room with them. 'Dad. why didn't you talk about your brother? What has he got to hide? Or what have you got to hide? Are you out there now looking for Peter? Is that what this is all about?'

Tears streamed down her face as she continued speaking to the ghost of her father.

'All through my childhood neither you nor Mum ever mentioned an uncle. Any normal father would have told me, would have let me meet him. Is he married? Has he any children? If so, I have cousins, an uncle I don't know, and you are a father I never knew.'

Her husband wrapped his arms around her and held her until there were no more tears.

'Joyce, you're tired, we're both tired. We'll go to bed, sleep on it, and start again tomorrow.'

She nodded and crept quietly up the stairs.

By the time Venning climbed into bed Joyce's breathing was deep and steady, but his mind was too active for sleep. What did Group Captain Dadswell know? Where was Peter Pringle? Why did the photograph album and the diary both end with Oradour-sur-Glane? And why was a man so obsessed with war loath to talk about it?

THREE

On the following morning, a wet Sunday morning, they returned to Oxford intending to sift through the papers, but Judith had other ideas.

'You said you'd take me to the Cotswold Wild Life Park today to do some brass rubbings.'

'Did I?'

'Yes, Daddy, you did.'

'It's far too wet, not only that your mother and I have some work to do. You could help, so why don't we do a deal?'

'What sort of deal?'

'We all work today, and next Sunday I'll take you up to London. We'll catch a river bus from Westminster Bridge to the Tower of London, spend the morning at The Tower, the afternoon at Madame Tussaud's then return home, tired out and eady for bed. Is that fair?'

She thought about it, eyeing her father doubtfully. 'Even if it's raining?'

'Yes, even if it's raining.'

'Okay, it's a deal.'

By tea time the material had been sorted into four piles, all in date order. 1921-1938; 1939-1945; 1946-1970; 1971 to June 1985 where everything stopped. They newspaper cuttings were kept separately in a box lid.. The first pile contained everything relating to Andrew's childhood; school reports; a certificate for swimming 200 yards in Midsummer Meadow Baths; photographs which proved conclusively that Andrew and Peter Pringle were identical twins; the two boys taken with their classmates at school; on the beach with their mother;

on the beach with their father; in a paddle boat; on their bicycles, and always laughing. In the second pile, 1939-1945, there were more photographs of the brothers, this time in the uniform of the Royal Air Force. They quickly developed from sheepish looking raw recruits into men who knew they had a purpose. On the sleeve of one were three stripes, on the other a single band. Julian and Joyce peered at the pencilled notes on the reverse. Sergeant Peter Pringle and Pilot Officer Andrew Pringle, January 1941. Another badly focussed snap dated March, 1941, showed them standing beside a plane with a panda painted on the side, and later, in July 1941, sitting in a pub with six of their friends, all with their glasses raised.

'It's a pity, Joyce, we don't know what they were celebrating.'

Several more snaps of the same crew taken between 1942 and 1943, with Andrew depicted in the centre, caught the men as they arrived home or as they were about to take off, but by 1944 things had changed. Peter stood with another six airmen, no smile on his face, looking drawn and tired. Julian wondered whether Andrew was the photographer. In the last photograph the men were gazing upwards. What had caught their attention? This was a far more professional piece of work which showed every detail clearly. In Andrew's right hand he clutched his flying helmet and the left was pressed to his head as though he was trying to disperse the world's worst headache.

'It's not a headache,' said Joyce suddenly. 'It's bad news. He stood exactly like that, his hand pressed to his head, when we heard my grandmother had died. He was heart broken, but it was the only sign he ever gave. How I wish he'd talked to me. Why on earth did he have to bottle everything up?'

'I've no idea, my darling. I hardly knew him, and neither did you, it seems. Let's read the letters, perhaps they'll give us a lead.'

'I doubt it. They're all so short, just one page using both sides, all signed by Andrew, with Peter squiggling a postscript.'

'God what a scrawl! Now, my darling. Let's see if we can decipher this one.'

April 1943
Dear Mum and Dad,
Thanks for your last long letter. It took us three days to read it! Don't worry, we're both fine. You'll be pleased to hear that Peter is no longer an observer, his new title is navigator. Can't fully explain his new duties, it's all hush-hush at the moment, but I can tell you that he doesn't have to act as front gunner any more or release bombs. He has his own small cubicle within the craft, and lots of switches to play with. I'm in sick bay for a few days, a real rest giving me time to catch up on my reading. I had a slight argument with a Messerschmidt 109 which has left me with shrapnel in my right arm and back, but none, fortunately, in my face. It's a funny business, this shrapnel, the doc who can only remove a bit at a time has to wait until it comes to the surface which means I'll have to return to sick bay every few weeks, Still I can't grumble, I'm still beautiful, so too are the nurses.
You asked in your last letter about our friends. We don't want friends, Mum. We don't want to get too close to each other. We don't want to mourn. Pete and I have each other, and we tend to stick with our own aircrew. If we go, and I know it sounds maudlin, we all go together. But don't worry, Mum, it helps to have my telepathic brother with me, You know what they say, together invincible, divided they fall, or something like that. Pete will be down to see you

on a flying visit next week. Don't save any of your rations for him. He'll bring some goodies with him. I think he's got a pal in the NAAFI with lovely legs. Not my type, though, and don't worry about us, we're flying high.
Love from us both, Andrew.
P.S. Arriving Wednesday, Peter. X X X X

'How extraordinary,' said Joyce. 'Doesn't sound like Dad at all, there's great humour which we never saw, and fun and ebullience. Peter's a bit lazy, isn't he, never more than the odd sentence.'

'I don't find it odd. With identical twins you nearly always find one leads, the other follows.'

An envelope yellow with age fell on the floor. Julian retrieved it and held it out to Joyce. 'Recognise the writing?'

'Yes, of course I do. That's my grandmother's scrawl. She enjoyed writing letters, wrote to us every week, four or five pages, but this isn't one of her lengthy ones. Look, only a page.'

'You decipher it, too spidery for me.'

Joyce read it aloud, slowly.
'My dear Andrew and Peter,
We're glad, Dad and I, that you've both been accepted for aircrew which is what you wanted, but it's sad to learn that you'll be parted so soon. It is difficult to believe Andrew will shortly be in Canada and you Peter buckling down to hard work at Padgate and that by the end of your training you will both be sergeants. Dad thinks becoming sergeants is rapid promotion but I'm afraid my Fabian soul was affronted by the implications. Reading between the lines leads me to believe that Northampton Grammar School wasn't good enough and that neither of you bright scholarship boys can ever expect to be commissioned officers. Andrew, it seems, is capable of becoming a sergeant pilot and skipper of his plane, and quite capable

of giving orders to commissioned officers flying with him, but not capable of sitting down in the officers' mess and passing the port in the right direction. Is it really necessary to go to Eton or Harrow to learn how to wield a knife and fork? And is this the sort of country my two boys will be fighting for. Dad tells me not to get so wound up, but it seems to me that the School Certificate is the same exam whether it's taken at Eton or Northampton Grammar School. You do all speak the same language I take it?
Half a minute, Dad is saying something. P A U S E. It's nothing to worry about, he's saying the same thing he always says when I get the bit between my teeth. "You're like an old dog with a bone," but old dog or not this is something I can't and won't ever forgive.
Do make the most of your last few days together. We think of you all the time.
      Love, Mum and Dad   X X X X X X
PS. The air raid sirens went this morning but I think they must have been practising. It really is a ghastly noise, turns my stomach over, but I guess we'll get used to it.

'Good old Gran,' said Joyce. She was right wasn't she?'

'It was another age, my darling. I'd no idea class was so important.' They read through the letters systematically.

'When you've read one,' said Joyce, 'you've read the lot. They all say again and again we're happy, and not to worry. They're not telling us anything.'

'Don't be too sure. Listen to this one dated May 4th 1943.
Dear Mum and Dad,
Yesterday was a black day. They won't let us fly together any more. Stupid really, because we can read each other's minds, no need for the indecision thatso often occurs. However, we are still attached to the same squadron of Lancasters at Waddington which means we can at least spend our leisure hours together. We play football once a

week which gives us the exercise we need after being cooped up in a flying machine. Pete's now playing left back and I remain in my old position at centre forward. We're still the unbeatable ping-pong duo and proud to announce that we haven't bought our own beer for yonks! Glad to hear Dad's rheumatism has eased, now look after yourselves, and don't worry about us.
Have just been made a pilot officer, but Pete says he draws the line at saluting me!
Love from us both, Andrew.
PS. What do we do now, Mum? We've both got our eyes on the same girl! Love, Peter.

'Reading between the lines, mutteed Julian, 'I'd say that this was the dividing of the ways. Did they quarrel over this girl, or did they learn to live without each other once they were in different aircraft?'

'All we have to do, darling, is read on.'

'Don't you think it's time you made coffee?'

'Hey! You're not in the Police Station now giving orders to your minions.'

He laughed. 'Okay, okay I'll make it.'

'Hang on, Julian, just read this.'

August 6th 1943
Dear Mum and Dad,
Sorry we missed sending our weekly letter, but you will have heard all about Operation Gomorrah, the term used for the Hamburg raids .They are not something to be kept under wraps since the press and radio have been spewing out all the details, real and imaginary, so there's no harm in telling you the story from our angle.
Of the 791 bombers despatched from Britain 740 actually bombed the target so ignore all those inaccurate headlines you're reading. The raid which was a long one lasted two and a half hours, during which

time we dropped well over 2000 tons of bombs and incendiaries as well as a packet of metallic strips we were given at the last minute. We'd no idea what they were for, but this surprise packet turned out to be magic, pure magic, and effectively mucked up the German radar. When we got back to base we heard that the boffins who'd invented this conjuring trick called it WINDOW. The master race, thank God, was all at sixes and sevens. Their searchlights, were all over the shoot, never once being able to focus on us.

The newspapers have been full of the damage to property, industry, and the submarine pens, but the all important first step was to cut the gas, water, and electricity mains and telephone lines. We also destroyed police, and fire headquarters which meant the following raids were even more devastating. As soon as we got back to base and put our heads down the Americans carried out a short daylight raid with 68 bombers. We all spent the next day on the base checking our planes and carrying out any necessary maintenance before striking again on the night of the 27/28th. This time 739 bombers dropped nearly two and a half thousand tons, and two nights later we went in again and dropped another 2382 tons. The third time was uncomfortably hot. The intense heat rising above the stricken city seemed to roast us as we flew. We were told it was imagination, probably true because our crate is as cold as an icebox, but I have never felt so warm in my life. Our cameras showed some amazing shots of a colossal firestorm, the like of which, so we're told, has never been witnessed before. Mature trees were uprooted, and thrown around like match sticks, and many unfortunate inhabitants were lifted off their feet and flung alive into the flames by winds gusting to well over 150 miles an hour. Air raid shelters became tombs as their bodies were incinerated by the consuming heat. Some people, so the German radio has been saying, were saved by jumping into canals and rivers and remaining there for hours and hours until the heat had subsided. It's not an action that bears thinking about, but thank

God we can't think about it while we're in the air. We're too busy concentrating on finding the target, avoiding the fighters, steering clear of the searchlights and the ack-ack, keeping a safe distance from our own planes, listening to instructions on the R/T, and always a watchful eye on the fuel gauge. The last raid on August 2/3 was the worst because the weather was atrocious, heavy cloud cover made the target virtually impossible to see and the storm force winds played havoc with the aircraft. Stirlings and Halifaxes were grounded, a few Wellingtons went out piloted by Polish squadrons whose hatred for the Germans spurs them on to perform unbelievable feats, but the bulk of the force was composed mainly of our splendid Lancasters because they can fly at well over 20,000 feet. It was an appalling night, Armageddon couldn't be worse. Operation Gomorrah was a victory no one cared to celebrate, we'd lost too many good friends.
We'll both be home for a couple of days the week after next. Keep the kettle boiling. Look after yourselves, we miss you.
Love Andrew and Pete

'How awful! How could my father have lived through that, and not talk about it?'

'Perhaps he was thinking of the 40,00 people who perished?'

'How did you know that?'

'I did modern history for my 'A' levels, but it never seemed real, until now. Come on Joyce, don't think about it, we've got to go on.'

It was the last letter which stunned them, the last letter home Andrew ever wrote.

April 3rd 1945.
Dear Mum and Dad,
I don't know how to begin, because this is something I should be saying to you, not writing, but Group Captain has ordered an enquirythat will take place in the morning, and I have to be there.

How do I tell you? I'm sorry, but there is only one way to say it. I would like to find words, words that aren't so final, but I never thought I'd have to write and say this. Peter is dead. Three words! How can three words say it all? He died at 3.30 this morning. No, it was worse than that. He didn't just die, he was murdered, that's what it was, murder by a bloody kraut in a rogue Junkers 88 that infiltrated into the midst of our pack after a raid on Rotterdam. We were all funnelling ready to land, Pete was in the second plane home and I was in the fifth. The Junkers was spotted and we were immediately given orders to disperse, but for Pete it was too late, his plane with its undercarriage already down, received a direct hit and exploded in mid air before crashing on the runway. We were told to land at Hemswell, but I ignored the order, ceased transmission with the ground, turned to pursue the bastard. A bloody stupid thing to do because a Lancaster can't keep up with a Junkers. It was only as I reached the coast that I came to my senses and realised how desperately short of fuel we were and how insane it was to risk the lives of my crew. However, there will come other days when I can repay this debt with interest. Don't cry, Mum. I'll come down as soon as I can. Never forget how Pete has enjoyed the last five years. "Better than work," he was always saying, but without him life will never be the same again, not for any of us.
Love, lots of love, Andrew.

Joyce buried her face in a cushion and wept.

'Come on my love, drink this brandy and don't cry. Our job now is to find him.'

'I can't help it. This is why he's never talked about the war. He wanted to forget. He had to forget.'

As she took a sip of brandy her thoughts returned to the conversation she'd heard as a child, when she'd crept down the stairs for a glass of water. If only they had talked to me, shared things with me, I would never have left home so early, and taken a job I didn't enjoy.'

'No, Julian, he didn't want to forget,' she shouted.

'What are you saying?'

'Vengeance, that's what I heard him say to Mother once. She told him not to be so stupid, that he wasn't alone with his grief, hundreds of others had also lost dear ones.'

'It's a long, long, time, Joyce, nearly half a century of time. He won't be wanting vengeance now. The German pilot may have been killed during the war, and if he was lucky enough to survive he'd be an old man now, in his 70's.'

'They looked pretty fit to me.'

'Who did?'

'Those Germans in that newspaper cutting, taken at Hendon. It's in the last pile.' She grabbed the few cuttings, and with a shout of triumph produced the cutting from *The Times* dated Saturday, April 25th, 1987.

'That's it, *Operation Giselle*, it could be any of those men pictured there.'

'Don't be crazy. You don't seriously think your father's gone off to Germany, knife in hand, to hunt for the man who shot down his brother's plane in 1944, and when he finds him, kill him?'

'No, not when you put it like that....it's too...too fanciful.

'Tomorrow, my love, when Judith has gone to school we'll go through his diaries and his notes with a fine tooth comb. The notes like his letters should be revealing, but right now we're going to relax. Relax! An impossibility for Detective Inspector Julian Venning who mulled over the case during dinner, all through a repeat of *Morse* on the box, in his bath and finally in bed. By the time he dropped off to sleep his modus operandi was complete. Joyce might not be too pleased but with only six weeks respite from DHQ his way was the only way.

The following morning he waited until Judith and Isabelle, her friend from next door but one, had tripped happily off to school before making another pot of coffee and taking it into the garden.

'Come and sit down, Joyce, and listen.'

'I thought we were going to get stuck into reading the notes.'

'We are eventually.'

'What does that mean?'

'If we are to find your father we must know why the diary stops at Limoges, and the only way to do that is to go there. Why don't you ask Mrs Clarke if Judith could stay over with Isabelle for a few days?'

'Of course she'll have Judith. She owes me. Didn't we have Isabelle here when Sheila had a hysterectomy? Farming Judith out isn't a problem, but you're rushing me Julian. We haven't even discussed it.'

'You couldn't. You were asleep. Are you prepared to come with me, or am I going alone?'

'No, of course you're not, but I still think we should have discussed it. Is this what you do at the station? Tell your men what to do without any discussion whatsoever?'

'It's the way I work, Joyce, but you don't have to come along.'

'I am coming, believe me!.'

'Good. Providing there's space on board for the car, we'll catch the Portsmouth Le Havre ferry tonight. We'll follow the same route as your father, stay in the same hotels, ask a lot of questions. All this may take anything up to a week. After that I'll see you safely on to a plane home from Orly, before driving to Berlin and calling on that supercilious RAF Officer to get some sense out of him.'

Joyce pulled a face. 'Isn't there any other way?'

'No, my darling, there isn't. You'll need to be here in case your father returns. If he does, ring me immediately and I'll be back within 24 hours.'

'What about the notes?'

'We'll read them en route, in the ferry, in the car, and by the time we reach Bernay we'll have a working knowledge of his background from the first pencilled note on the 10th August, 1939 up to the end of the war, and hopefully beyond.'

'What about booking hotels?'

'No problem. There's an up to date *Logis de France* in my briefcase. I picked it up at the French Tourist Office in Piccadilly when I was in town for a briefing at The Yard.' A vestige of a smile flitted across Joyce's face. 'Just in case we decided to holiday in France,' he said quickly.

'You are a dark horse.'

'No, I'm not, merely forgetful.'

Joyce laughed. 'All right, Machiavelli, tell me how you know that my father used hotels advertised in the *Logis*?

'Because I rose in the small hours to check. Each hotel mentioned in the diary is in the *Logis* and each one has a lift, an essential for someone in a wheelchair. There's no way your father could have lugged your mother up badly lit stairs with the lighting operating on a time-switch system which means you to have to press and run-like-hell, a method used by the majority of small French hotels. Good fun for the able bodied, all part of the genuine French atmosphere combined, of course, with a smell of garlic and gauloise, but not I think suitable for your father.'

'Jule, I'm beginning to look forward to this trip.'

'Good on you. Well, don't let's waste any more time. You go and see Mavis, while I make a few phone calls. He consulted the *Logis* before tapping out the number of a hotel in Bernay.

'Bonjour Madame, avez vous une chambre, avec un salle du bain, pour deux personnes, demain?'

'Oui, monsieur. Pouvez vous arrive avant six heures?'

'Oui, madame.'

'A bon. Votre nom monsieur, s'il vous plait?

It was easy. From Bernay, Chartres, Montlucon, and Limoges, the answer was the same. "Oui, monsiur, nous avons une chambre." With the hotels safely booked Julian rang P & O. He was in luck as far as the car was concerned, but out of luck when it came to accommodation. All the cabins had been reserved so he settled, instead, for two club class seats, comfortable enough to catnap on, and admirable when the time came to concentrate on the notebooks.

Sheila Clarke welcomed the idea of having Judith to stay. "Two are much easier than one," she confided, "and they play so happily together." Joyce returned to the house to collect all Judith's clobber and her much loved hairless teddy bear. As she pressed his tummy to see if he still squeaked she realised, for the first time since their marriage, that the two of them would be alone. There'd not been time for a honeymoon, a case had come between the idea and the reality. She made up her mind to enjoy the next few days, and the only way to do that was to thrust her father into the back of her mind. Not quite so easy as she thought.

FOUR

They stood on deck as the ferry eased its way out of harbour, passing naval ships, destroyers, frigates, and an aircraft carrier all dull grey, nameless but numbered, with no sign of life aboard. The Inspector, in his mind's eye, saw the harbour as his father would have seen it, fifty years before, when serving in minesweepers based at Portsmouth. A constant coming and going of every type of ship from M.T.B's to battleships, all looking to the signal stations for instruction. No radio-telephone, so his father had said, unless there was fog, then the message would be despatched in code. No good feeding information to the enemy. When two flags, I and J in the international code were hoist, *Item Jig* to the signalmen, ships were being given the go ahead to proceed in execution of previous orders, or the aldis lamp with its narrow angle of sight would relay a message in morse to a signalman on board a ship destined to depart. The signal stations must have been stretched, he thought, in the run-up to 'D' Day. Since the start of his holiday he'd never stopped thinking about a war he'd never known. Andrew Pringle had a lot to answer for!

The shore receded until all they could see were the lights of other ships in the Channel. Joyce sighed, contented and strangely happy despite the job ahead of them. 'Julian, do you realise.....'

'That this is the first time we've been alone since we left the Registry Office?'

'Yes.'

'There's only one answer to that. We must take our pleasures as they come, and treat the next four days as our long overdue honeymoon. We'll not stint ourselves, only the best will do.

Champagne right now, and Chablis and oysters when we arrive at Bernay.'

'Sounds heavenly, darling.'

An hour later they settled down in their club class seats to tackle the first of the notebooks. The champagne, or maybe the motion of the ship induced in Joyce a deep sleep, leaving her husband who was totally embroiled in the whereabouts of his missing father-in-law to carry on with the research alone. He patiently and methodically read through the four notebooks, and by 6 o' clock, an hour before the ship docked, a vivid picture of a family at war had emerged. The two boys joined up on August 10th 1939, and after medical examinations, and ability tests they were both accepted for aircrew. A week later their father found work in a munition factory, and their mother joined the Women's Voluntary Service. Andrew as a pilot-to-be was sent to a Flying Training School in Canada, and Peter who became an observer spent several weeks at Padgate, not too far from Warrington. Andrew, it seemed, didn't think much of the old crates used for training and longed to be back in England where he could fly a real plane, a Wellington. Peter, who'd always unquestioningly followed his elder brother, older by half an hour, was desperately miserable during their enforced separation, but by the time Andrew returned to England his young brother had become a competent front gunner observer whose responsibility also involved aiming bombs. During his training he'd found the centre of the target indicators with consumate ease and passed out top in his group. Andrew who also passed out with flying colours, those were his own words, was drafted to an airfield in Shropshire where he learned to handle Wellingtons. For him it was bliss, the Clee Hills, the Wrekin, Malverns, and

Cotswolds gave him a glimpse of the finest landscape he'd ever seen, not nearly as forbidding as The Rockies. When Andrew was ready to face the enemy he persuaded the C.O. in charge of training to post him to RAF Waddington where Peter was stationed. By the end of 1942 they were still in the same crew flying Manchesters. Later they transferred to Lancasters. "A heavenly heavy armed bomber which can reach the stars," again Andrew's actual words. Lancasters, Venning learnt, could fly at over 20,000 feet, light years away from Andrew's stars, but the writer's hyperbole was endearing.

There were several pages of descriptions of raids on Dortmund, Frankfurt, Bremen, and Dusseldorf, but the most telling accounts were of raids on Essen and Hamburg. The notes, extraordinarily visual, were written with great clarity. Transported back in time, Venning found it easy to re-live, vicariously, a raid on Essen, far more informative than all the books he'd read because here was a personal story from a man he knew. Andrew frequently referred to his Lancaster as my mermaid, a figure, painted on the side of the hatch which Venning remembered seeing in one of the old photographs. Mermaid, it seemed, had been badly damaged, and the fitters working round the clock had performed miracles. Work which would have taken a week in peacetime took exactly five hours. According to Andrew aircrews never knew their objective until the briefing, which resulted in a lively betting shop on the base, with one of the armourers acting as banker. Andrew and his crew always placed bets, but never took wild guesses. They didn't have to, because they knew the plane's tanks, situated in the wings, were capable of storing 2,500 gallons. All they did, once they knew the load, was to estimate the distance. Occasionally, very occasionally, they were right!

For the Essen raid the Mermaid carried twelve 500 pound demolition bombs and a blast bomb weighing 4,000 pounds, known as Cookie. The briefing, prior to the engagement, for engagement there would be with the enemy's night fighters, always followed the same pattern. First the Met man warned them of icing levels, at 5,000 feet, and broken cloud cover over the target, followed by the Flying Control Officer who was responsible for getting two squadrons of 40 planes airborne, then the Intelligence Officer gave them the positions of marker flares en route, and German night fighter bases. Their Squadron Leader warned them about decoy fires and finally when the Station Commander and Navigation Leader had finished, all watches were synchronised.

After the briefing crews were kitted out. They collected their parachutes which had been checked, donned their sheepskin jackets and fur lined boots, never forgetting to wear silk socks which helped them withstand the bitter cold in unheated aircraft. "On the journey to Essen," Andrew had recorded, "the temperature at 20,000 feet was minus 40 degrees centigrade." Julian wondered how they managed to think and operate in such conditions. At this point Andrew had changed from pencil to ink and the notes became easier to read. "Essen was our 27th operation together, now we've only three more to go before the end of the tour and ten days leave. God willing, Pete and I will be able to play some tennis, and maybe get in a little fishing."

As he read the description of the two squadrons taxying down to the runway, bombed up and ready to go, Venning found it easy to see plane after plane, nose to tail, with their complement of airmen making last minute checks; pressures and temperature; bomb doors closed; hydraulic brake pressure; trim, propeller, fuel and flaps all in order. The slightest thing missed might mean the difference between life and death. As the planes reached the runway a beam from an aldis lamp changed from red to green giving each plane a signal for take off. Total radio silence prevailed, always total silence when they were under way.

Andrew's scrawl at this point was difficult to decipher but it looked as if he had written *It was like cutting the umbilical cord. We were on our own. Thank God, for Gee.*
What the hell was Gee? Maybe he'd pick that up further on?

It took forty minutes for us to climb to our ceiling, and then we cruised at 200 miles an hour. The engines worried me, they were making more racket then usual. I prayed we'd get back in one piece. Before we reached the target, Tim, our navigator reported fires and spoof red and green markers, but Gee told us clearly we were not on target.

Must be some sort of navigation aid, mused Venning.
We wouldn't have been fooled by the markers, the Krauts can never place them high enough, neither can they produce a convincing red. Ten minutes later we had the aiming point in our sights, Cookie went first, and photographs later showed it was bang on, so too were the 500 pounders. The marshalling yards at Essen didn't know what had hit them, or perhaps they did. They were a write off, well for some weeks anyway, and the three trains carrying ammunition provided the most exciting firework display I've ever seen. Guy Fawkes would have been proud of us.

By 4 a.m. Julian was stuck well into the third notebook. For the past two hours he'd been thinking what a splendid book could be structured from the notes, but rapidly changed his mind when he came to the description of Peter's death that produced in Andrew a deeply felt rancorous hatred, paranoeic in the extreme inciting him to murder..

Nothing, nothing can ever be the same again. I promise you, Peter, that I will bloody find this murdering bastard, no matter how long it takes, but he will pay. Oh yes, dear brother, he will pay.

The police inspector who had never read a diary to compare with what he had in his hand was even more astounded as he began to read through the fourth notebook. Andrew now out of the RAF and working in the Legal Department was bitter about the way Bomber Command had been treated at the end of the war.

8525 bombers and their crews destroyed, he had written. *47268 men in all shamefully treated by the country for which they fought. Snubbed by the British Government who refused to sanction a campaign medal for Bomber Command's offensive against Germany on the slender premise that aircrews operated from Britain which was not an official theatre of war. A bloody joke, Pete. Your life thrown away, not even worth an inscription on a pennyworth of metal.*

He was also vitriolic in his condemnation of anything German. The long passages of hatred and promises of retribution were interlaced with wondrous descriptions of operas he'd seen or heard, and occasional notes about Joyce. Emily, it seemed, persistently refused to holiday abroad, but this didn't deter Andrew. He was all set to go on an office trip to Trier, in Germany, when Emily collapsed. There was no option but to remain at home and look after her. Gradually the venomous passages became fewer until they ceased altogether, and gardening and opera took over. Only then did Emily relent and agree to a continental holiday. They went to France for three weeks, and the notes like the diary ended on the fourth day when they stayed in Limoges and visited a village called Oradour-sur-Glane. Julian knew, intuitively, that somewhere in that ruined village they would discover the reason for Andrew's strange behaviour. Joyce was still fast asleep. Just as well. He didn't really want her to learn more about her father or read the notebooks in depth. He'd tell her all she needed to know.

They disembarked at Le Havre shortly after 7 a.m. and drove leisurely through Normandy towards Pont de Tancarville, a vast toll bridge over the Seine which dominates the countryside. Shortly afterwards they crossed the Risle at Pont Audemer and took the road to Bernay. At 8.30 being decidedly peckish they stopped at St Denis-des-Monts for croissants and coffee.

'We should do this more often,' laughed Joyce.

'Well there's tomorrow and tomorrow and tomorrow, or should I say demain?'

'I wonder if Dad stopped off here?'

'We'll never know because your father only recorded hotels, and visits to the Cathedral at Chartres, and Oradour sur Glane.'

Joyce appeared to be engrossed in the efforts of a group of old men who were playing boule on a dusty expanse outside the cafe, but her mind was elsewhere. 'It was war, wasn't it,' she said suddenly, 'they were killing each other?'

'Of course it was war. What are you getting at?'

'The German pilot in the Junkers, the pilot who shot Peter down was obeying orders, he's no more a murderer than the next man. He must have had guts tucking himself into a squadron of enemy aircraft. How on earth did he manage it?'

'That's crossed my mind. The first problem, and the most difficult, I imagine, would be to pick up the right speed, then he'd have to rely on cloud cover to slink into the pack. I can't believe that anyone carrying out a mission like that ever expected to see Germany again.'

'Maybe he didn't.'

'That's more than possible with our fighters and ack-ack gunning for him.'

'Why couldn't Dad understand it was an eye for an eye?'

'I'm sure it has something to do with being a twin.'

'But Dad could have been given the same orders. Get out there to Hanover, or wherever, and dive bomb them on the ground.'

'I don't think dive bombing was our style, Japanese and German maybe, but not British for some inexplicable reason.'

'But,' persisted Joyce, 'If Dad had been given orders he would have obeyed.'

'Yes, yes, I guess he would.'

It was late afternoon when they arrived at the hotel where the buxom Madame greeted them with a smile. She was astonished, in truly Gallic fashion, at monsieur's command of the French language. When Julian explained he'd studied French and German for his degree she sat them down, produced a bottle of cognac, and regaled them with stories of her grandfather, an Englishman, who never returned to England after the First World War. Joyce hardly understood a word, but it was all too clear to the inspector that as soon as any English guests arrived, with the gift of tongues, Madame sat them down and told the same stories again and again.

'Madame,' he asked, in his impeccable French, 'do you, by any chance, remember an English couple who spent the night here five years ago? The wife was in a wheelchair, and they arrived by car.'

Madame wrinkled her nose, and shook her head.'We often have wheelchairs, monsieur, it is very difficult.'

Venning produced a snapshot. 'It's not very good, Madame, but it may help.'

She peered at it for some moments. 'Ah, monsieur, I think I remember them though I have forgotten their name.'

'Pringle, Mr and Mrs Andrew Pringle.'

'Mais oui, the poor woman had a great sense of humour for one so disabled. They weren't here long, just the one night, and I remember them sitting right here after dinner playing a word game.'

'Scrabble?'

'Yes, that's it, monsieur. Very serious they were too. They went to bed early, tired I dare say after a day's travelling. Ah, mon dieu, how could I have forgotten! Madame Pringle was very gracious, she gave me a tin of biscuits, your Scottish shortbread.'

'Where did they go?'

'I've no idea, monsieur. Five years in the life of a hotel is a long time, but why do you want to know, monsieur?'

'Mr Pringle is my wife's father and we thought it might be an interesting exercise to follow the same route.'

Madame looked puzzled. 'But why didn't you ask him?'

'We will, madame, when we see him again.'

Oysters were not on the menu. Instead they settled for *moules mariniere* with a fine 1985 Chablis. They too went to bed early, leaving a *Please don't disturb* notice on the door. Bliss for them both. Bliss knowing the phone wouldn't ring. Bliss knowing they had all the time in the world. For a few brief hours their entire world was centred in a double bed in a small French town, where their only thoughts were for each other.

After a late breakfast they bade au revoir to madame, and pointed the car in the direction of Chartres. They were 40 miles away when they saw the magnificent Gothic cathedral rising out of the flat Normandy countryside.

'You've been here before, Julian, but you never told me it would be anything like this. Sends tingles down my spine.'

'Well, I'm betting those tingles will reach your toes by the time we get inside.'

Joyce had never ever experienced anything like it before. The sound of choral singing greeted them as they stepped through the west door into the past, leaving the modern world behind. The sun, too bright outside without dark glasses, streamed through the stained glass windows lighting the interior with myriad colours. She shivered slightly. It was, in a strange way despite its beauty, quite awe inspiring.

'Julian,' she whispered, 'I do hope Dad heard the singing, and I hope the sun shone like this when he pushed Mum round.'

The Frenchwoman who greeted them at the *Du Boeuf Couronne* was fairly new to the job. She'd no recollection of seeing the Pringles, but she'd ask monsieur to have a word with them during the evening. Monsieur couldn't remember them either, but he did produce his records for 1985 and as he leafed through June gave a grunt of satisfaction when he found Andrew's signature.

'Juin, dix neuf cent quatre vingt cinq. Voilà le nom de votre père, Madame Venning, mais il est resté ici une nuit seulement. Ah oui,' he said pointing to a pencilled note, 'le fauteuil roulant, votre mère était avec lui.'

'What does that mean, Julian?'

'Wheelchair!'

The proprietor of *Le Fiacre*, in Montlucon, lifted his arms and his eyes to the heavens in truly Gallic fashion. 'Rappeler!, monsieur! Depuis cinq ans. C'est impossible. Le monde arrive ici. 'Ow, monsieur, should I remember?'

Monsieur Froissart was in no mood to answer such stupid questions. He had more pressing domestic problems. The chef married to his eldest daughter had, after a blistering row on the previous evening, upped and left. Now he, the proprietor, would have to take over the kitchen, something he hadn't done in years. 'C'est la vie, c'est la vie,' he muttered to himself as he handed the visitors their room key. The news percolated through to the hotel guests as news mostly does, but it added another dimension to the five course evening meal. Would the soupe julienne be too filling, the dressing on the escargots piquant, the beef saignant, the Roquefort mature, and the fraises au porto sweet enough? After two hours of tasting the delights of the proprietor's cuisine to the accompaniment of a Chateau Neuf du Pape 1982, and a Beaumes de Venise they awarded him an alpha plus. After coffee they strolled slowly round the town, before retiring for the night the reason for their journey forgotten and sleep not their objective, which is why they overslept and didn't leave Montlucon until noon.

Limoges fascinated Joyce. Shop after shop full of delicate china. She bought several miniature pieces, a grand piano and stool, a vase, a table and chairs all for Judith's doll's house. Venning encouraged his wife to wander round the town, look at the sights and enjoy the atmosphere while she could. Oradour could wait until the morrow, giving them a chance to talk to the proprietor of the hotel. Dinner was a leisurely affair lasting two hours during which time they downed three carafes of local wine. When the meal was over Venning tackled Madame who was loath to talk about previous guests. Once she learnt that Emily was dead and Andrew missing she softened considerably, sighed, and sat down at their table prepared to tell all, in a slow halting English.

'They were both very happy when they arrived because your mother had succeeded in walking in the little park near here.'

'Mother walked!'

'Yes, not too far, from one seat to the next, but your father was pleased with her progress. On the first night they really enjoyed their dinner. I remember it quite clearly because your mother who'd never eaten escargots before decided to try them.'

'Did she enjoy them?'

'Mais oui. After dinner your father reserved their room for a few more days, and asked me to recommend any places of interest they could visit with a wheelchair. I suggested, as I do to all travellers, a visit to the Village of the Martyrs.'

'Village of the Martyrs,' said Joyce quietly. 'Where's that?'

'At Oradour-sur-Glane, madame, not Oradour-sur-Vayres.

The next day they left the hotel shortly after lunch. Your mother, holding on to your father's arm, managed to walk the short distance to the car. He folded the wheelchair, and put it in the boot, and off they went happy and smiling.' She paused, looked at the Julian and shook her head.

'Carry on, madame, please.'

'It's something I shall never understand. They were not French, they had no relatives here, they lost no one, and yet on their return from Oradour they were two different people. I didn't see them until dinner, but your mother, no longer smiling and joking was silent, and your father who hardly ate a morsel, sat staring out of the window as though he'd seen a ghost. None of our visitors to Oradour has ever been so affected, red eyes, yes, but not stunned into total silence. But the strangest, weirdest thing of all, was what happened to your mother...she could no longer walk.'

Tears streamed down Joyce's face. 'Come on, my love, you're tired. It's time for bed. We'll discuss it in the morning.'

As Madam moved to the next table shook her head. What wa it about Oradour that had given these two families so much grief.

'She could no longer walk! whispered Joyce as she climbed into bed. Why Julian, why?

'I have no idea, my darling. Let's try and get some shut-eye.'

Only in the small hours did they manage to sleep hence a late breakfast that also served as lunch.

Early in the afternoon they drove to the Village of the Martyrs following Andrew's pattern in every respect. Even the weather was the same, a relentless sun in a cloudless sky became too hot for comfort. So it was, on the 10th June 1944, when the quiet agricultural village of Oradour became the target for a vengeful German dictator. Venning parked outside the gates fully expecting to pay both a parking and entrance fee, but the French have eschewed commercialism. This shrine of remembrance is tastefully preserved and treated with reverence and respect. Silence is all they ask, but there's no need, for the enormity of what happened at Oradour silences everyone who visits the village. In two hours on a sunny afternoon, forty-five years ago, 642 villagers were massacred.

The silence was uncanny. If visitors spoke at all, they spoke in whispers. Everyone walked softly through this village where all the women and children had been herded into the church and burnt alive, the imprint of their bodies still visible on the walls. One woman escaped, but how wondered Venning, did she live with the memory? One child, a refugee from Alsace, escaped by leaping through a classroom window, and was away across the fields before the headmaster, who believed the Germans were making a routine check, could stop him. The men were lined up against a wall and shot. The same treatment for all including the doctor, the gendarme, the priest, the postmaster, and the notary. Invalids were shot in their beds and cremated in their own homes. Only a handful of men working in the fields and two women shopping in Limoges were spared.

'It's eerie,' said Joyce in a whisper. 'In this bright sun it looks like a film set. Trolley tracks with overhead cables hanging loose, a school, post office, shops and church, even the doctor's car standing burnt out in his front garden. I can't believe it happened. Let's get away, Julian, I can't take any more.'

'OK, darling. You go back to the car. I want to take a look at the cenotaph, find out exactly where Andrew was standing when he took the photograph.'

'Is that important?'

'It might be.'

Venning noticed men taking off their hats as they walked past the vast communal tomb, some stopped, crossed themselves, and said a prayer for the dead. A lone woman knelt on the grass beside the tomb, a rosary in her hand. He followed the crowd into the cemetery and after reading many of the names on the wall his attention was drawn to a large family grave some distance from the cenotaph. At last he was able to stand where Andrew had stood when he took the photograph.

He glanced down at the grave with its porcelain flowers, and then at the family photographs on the headstone. A mother, a young mother with her six little girls, aged from one year to seven years, had all perished in the holocaust in the church. The physical pain he felt was indescribable. At last he knew what had happened to Andrew on a sunny afternoon in June 1985. Now he had to find him, and quickly, before it was too late.

FIVE

Andrew Pringle now a proficient German speaker shoved the piece of paper, Ed Watkins had laughingly called a certificate of merit, into an old illustrated copy of *Pilgrim's Progress*. That piece of paper, he knew, would give the game away. He must do the job properly, hide his tracks, no way must anyone find him until the job was done. There was no need to worry about Joyce any more, she was married now, and that policeman husband of hers was a caring man, intelligent too, that's why since Emily's death, Andrew had decided to keep himself to himself. No one was going to obstruct him this time.

Care! Care was all that was needed. Leave the car in the garage. Don't book through local travel agents. Take a bus to the station at Milton Keynes, a busy place where no one would remember him. Pay by cash, no cheques, or cheque cards. Get down to London, find a Thomas Cook's, book a night ferry from Harwich to Amsterdam. Spend a day in Amsterdam unwinding, then a flight to West Berlin, but there had been a fly in the ointment. Ron had insisted on driving him to Heathrow, but he had managed to concoct a story near enough to the truth. Something he had always wanted to do was see a performance of *Rigoletto* in the Baths at Caracalla. He'd never see it now — it was a dream, but Ron didn't have to know that. Instead of boarding a plane to Rome he had gone to Berlin via Paris, and not via Amsterdam as originally planned, but it would work.

He'd had it all mapped out for weeks. He'd done his homework. Studied Hallwag's map, read Fodor's Guide from cover to cover, seen a travel film, paid £23.50 for a photographic record of *Old and New Berlin*, which he didn't begrudge. A fascinating study. Pictures of the 1936 Olympic Games in a massive stadium where the architect of the 3rd Reich had sat foaming at the mouth as he watched Jesse Owens storming home to victory after victory. The man with three gold medals was snubbed by the Führer who refused to shake hands with a black athlete. What, mused Andrew, would the Führer have made of the Christies, Jacksons, Regises, and Daley Thompsons of today? And what will I make of Berlin a place I've never set foot in although I've been there as an avenging angel often enough? Sometimes on a clear night, Berlin,surrounded by rivers, lakes, and canals had looked like a city rising out of the water. At other times the cloud cover had been so extensive that they'd hardly seen anything until the last moment when the red and green markers had guided them to an almost invisible target. His present target was also invisible. Would the Group Captain stationed at Gatow be able to fire accurate markers?

The Air France flight landed dead on time at Berlin Tegel. A grey-haired seventy-year old Englishman in a nondescript suit, that no one was likely to remember, strode straight through customs and passport control without being challenged. He hopped on an airport bus into the centre of Berlin, then travelled by underground to Botanischer Garten only a stones' throw from the Hotel Ravenna where he had reserved accommodation. Andrew Pringle had not skimped. Why should he?No need to count the cost. In a few days or weeks money would have no meaning for him. Oblivion was his destination.

After a welcome soak in the bath he called Francis Dadswell but it was late in the afternoon before they made finally made contact. The Group Captain, who thanks to his brother was

expecting the call, said he was tied up with meetings all next day but softened the blow by inviting Andrew to join him at the opera house that evening for a performance by the resident company.
.

The applause was heartfelt and instantaneous as the final chorus from *Die Meistersinger von Nürnberg* echoed round the Deutsche Oper. As each of the soloists took their calls the applause increased until members of the audience no longer able to show their appreciation through mere clapping stamped their feet. By the time the conductor appeared centre stage to take his bow the air was thunderous with excitement and emotion.

Group Captain Dadswell glanced to his right and noticed with satisfaction that his guest, an avowed Verdi fanatic, was equally enthusiastic. After a slow final curtain, the houselights came up, and the audience, still bemused by a performance which had feasted their eyes, moved their hearts and assailed their ears with music they'd never forget, began leaving the theatre.

'Follow me, Andrew,' shouted Francis Dadswell, 'I know an excellent Bierkeller behind the theatre.'

'Are you free tomorrow evening?' shouted Andrew.

'Yes, why do you ask?'

'Have you any aversion to Verdi?'

'None whatsoever.'

Then hang on a jiffy while I get two tickets for *Un Ballo in Maschera.*'

The tavern, blessedly cool, after the heat of the theatre, filled rapidly with opera buffs still wound up with the erotic magical performance they'd just witnessed.

'Nuremburg, for me,' said Francis between sips of ice cold lager, 'is the most exciting of the Wagner operas because it's basic.'

'Basic! A strange description of an opera. In what way?' asked Andrew.

'It tells us about Wagner himself whom, I believe, identified with two roles, that of Walther who is refused admission to the Guild of Mastersingers because they don't understand his art, and Hans Sachs the enlightened shoe-maker poet who is bewitched by both Walther's music and his vision of a world without bigotry and violence. No cankers in Wagner's soul.'

'That's something I'm sure the Führer never recognised,' said Andrew bitterly. 'It isn't an opera I would have chosen but I'm glad you were so persuasive.'

'Why ever not?'

'Stupidity, I suppose. The word Nuremburg never fails to conjure up a totally different scene.'

'The trial was nearly half a century ago, best forgotten, it's history now.'

'Not for those families whose relations were annihilated in the concentration camps. They know that too many of the thugs who controlled those camps are not in Argentina, but in England, living among us, disguised beneath a cloak of respectability. Vengeance, retribution is what they seek, and at long last the matter has been raised in the House.'

'But ousted, Andrew, in The Lords and I agree with them. It doesn't do to pursue this type of vendetta. After four decades the evidence is sketchy, and memories faulty. After 45 years I would have found it difficult to recognise my own brother, and I'm totally convinced The Lords took the right line. The sight of old men and women, who may be innocent, being dragged into the dock to defend themselves against an overpowering hatred which has eaten up man's soul is anathema.'

Andrew nodded slightly-- best not to say anything more. He took another sip of his beer and looked at the grey and balding men in the Bierkeller, and wondered who'd been in the Gestapo, who in the SS, and who in the Luftwaffe.

'How about tomorrow, Andrew? Can you tear yourself away from the Staatsbibliothek for a couple of hours and join me for a bit of light relief between my many meetings?'

'What is it this time? Tennis or squash?'

'Neither. Every Wednesday morning I spend an hour or two on the range, occasionly blasting away with a Sterling sub-machine gun, but usually it's revolver practice to keep my eye in, so to speak.'

'If you can put up with a genuine tyro then I'd love to have a go. Haven't fired a revolver since the war.'

'Good man. Your company will be welcome. The lads think I'm a nutcase, but I enjoy the sport, gets me out of the office away from all the boring routine. I'll send a car to pick you up. The driver can go via the Olympic Stadium, Army HQ might interest you, and on Friday, Andrew, I'm looking forward to being introduced to *Un Ballo in Maschera*. Will Verdi stand up to Wagner, I wonder?'

'You're sure, are you, that your wife doesn't want to join us?'

'Quite sure. Angela hates opera, in fact she hates going to the theatre. Cinema, yes. Theatre, no. That's why your visit has given me so much pleasure. Now home, James, I suppose. I'll call a taxi and drop you on the way.'

'There's no need, Francis. You're going west and I'm going south, it's easy for me, and quicker, to take the underground to Botanischer Garten. The five minute walk to the hotel will do me good.'

'If that's what you want, my friend. From Opera you change at Zoologischer Garten. Tell me, what's the Ravenna like?'

'Excellent. Friendly management, and good food when I'm there which isn't often, thanks to you and Angela. I'll miss your company, Francis, but when I've finished reading the history of the Luftwaffe at the *Staatsbibliothek.* I'll be taking up your introductions in Freiburg, and hopefully doing some research in the *Militärgeschichtliches Forschungsamt* next week.'

'It has an enormous library, I believe, and like everything the Germans do, is highly organised. I'm sure Doctor Erlbach will do everything in his power to assist. I am certainly looking forward to seeing this book of yours published. You'll be giving me a signed copy, of course.'

'Of course!' murmured Andrew.'However, there is a great deal more research to do before I achieve what I've set out to do.'

'A perfectionist, that's what I like to hear.'

However, don't let's dwell on my problems, how about one for the road?' asked Andrew in an effort to change the direction of the conversation.

Forgive me, Andrew, if I make tracks, have just remembered that I've one or two problems to sort out before the morrow, but I'll look forward to seeing you on the range.'

Andrew closed the bedroom door behind him, and lay fully clothed on the bed. It was July 10th, three months to the day since Emily's death.

He stood once again, motionless, in the small crematorium chapel, his head bowed, as rollers inaudible under the music, carried away the coffin containing his wife's body.

It wasn't much of a send-off for you Emily, only three of us there
to give thanks for your life, and your memory. No one, not
even Joyce, remembers you as you were. Vivacious, beautiful, caring
and loving. No one else had such an irrepressible and infectious
giggle. Forgive me, Emily, for not becoming the man you thought
you'd married. I am sorry, but what damned good is it being sorry
now? It could all have been so different, if only...
You tried to divert me from my purpose, God knows, you tried, and
you so nearly succeeded. You were even getting better yourself, walking a little, developing strength in those legs, when there was a re-awakening of the old anger, a call for vengeance. Life for
life, eye for eye, tooth for tooth. Isn't that what the bible tells us? I heard the summons and you recognised the inevitable. The sun
should never shine, Emily. You know that, but something unforgiveable
happened that day, for you never walked again. Forgive me, my darling.

After the funeral Andrew spent hours in the garden, weeding, dead heading his roses. *Ena Harkness, Peace, and Frensha*. He then concentrated on cutting back a rambling rampant *Albertine* that had gone completely berserk and taken over the garage. Blast! It had happened again, always the beautiful but vicious *Albertine*. As he sat on the garden seat, squeezing out the thorn and sucking his thumb in an effort to clean the slight wound, he thought of Doc Lawson, who'd hummed a tuneless unrecognisable air while removing the damned shrapnel. Nearly fifty years ago, but it could have been yesterday. Two weeks after Pete's death he'd returned, for the third time, to sick bay for abstraction treatment. Chalmers, his old Squadron Leader, sat by his bed fiddling with the trophies of war, bits of shrapnel displayed on his bedside table. Chalmers was paying him a visit for a reason which had nothing to do with get-well-chum-camaraderie. Everyone knew how the Squadron Leader hated sick bay.

'You could play fives with this stuff, Andy, or knuckle bones as we called it at Stowe.' Chalmers picked up five pieces of shrapnel, threw them into the air catching three on his splayed out right hand, but not quick enough to prevent two bits falling on the floor. He fell on his knees and scrabbled around under the patient's bed.

'Stop fidgeting, Chalmers, leave them on the floor and say what you have to say.'

'All right, Andy, old son. Take it easy. Talked to Groupie last night, he's most concerned, asked me to come and see you.'

'There's nothing wrong with me, I'll be back on duty in a couple of days. It's only a bit of shrapnel, for heaven's sake.'

'I'm not here to talk about bloody shrapnel, it's about the way, old son, you've taken Pete's death.'

Andrew lay back on the pillow staring at the ceiling saying nothing. This riled the Squadron Leader who thought the Group Captain should have done his own dirty work.

'Listen to me, Pringle, we are professionals, and like the Germans we have a job to do. We're given a target to bomb and we bomb it. We don't start questioning the ethics of war. If we all did that we'd have the Krauts here on our doorstep and bloody Adolf Hitler living it up in Buckingham Palace.'

Andrew closed his eyes, even more annoying to the man trying to put his point across.

'You're not stupid, Pringle, you know what the Group Captain wants me to say to you. It's all this talk about retribution which is unsettling in a base like this. Describing Pete's death as cold blooded murder just won't do old son. Fortunes of war and all that. You've got to be philosophic about things, happens all the time. Supposing this German pilot had made several trips, and supposing he'd shot down six planes each with a complement of seven men, and supposing those men all had brothers in the RAF. It means you'd have forty two men all shouting the odds about the Krauts being murdering thugs. Doesn't make sense, old son.'

'And neither does your argument, Chalmers. You didn't see your brother killed, so you don't know what you're talking about.'

Poor Chalmers, who'd tried to help, was shot down two weeks later.

The ceiling had changed colour, it was now a soft green with concealed lighting. Andrew returned to the present marvelling at the elasticity of the mind which can go backwards and forwards at will. It was his twelfth night in the *Ravenna* a hotel that he'd chosen with care; easy to move around on the underground, convenient for Army HQ, and the State Library. He'd been welcomed by both the Dadswells, and to his surprise found that he and Francis had a lot in common. He'd no friends in England, didn't make friends easily, no ex-colleagues from the office, or members from the tennis club, no one in whom he'd ever wanted to confide. Now he felt guilty at not coming clean with Francis Dadswell. He had already lied to him, to the man who had referred to him as afriend. Researching a book, he'd told him, about the RAF. Incomplete without the qualifying Luftwaffe material. Will take some time. Francis had paved the way. Introduced him to the right people, delivered him to an erudite librarian in the Staatsbibliothek, where yesterday he'd struck gold. Reading through the vast history of Reichsmarschall Hermann Goering's Luftwaffe, which the marshal had confidently boasted would overpower the RAF, he came across a reference to *Operation Giselle*. With suppressed excitement he whispered the words to himself. *Launched in March 1945. A secret operation to destroy RAF bombers as they land at their home bases.* There was no more than that. Now he needed detailed information which meant a few days at the *Militargeschichtliches Forschungsamt* in Freiburg.

Andrew tilted backwards in his chair and relaxed which caused the German sitting at the same table in the reference library to wonder what it was in those heavy tomes on the history of the Luftwaffe which made the Englishman smile. The Englishman was not even thinking about the Luftwaffe, he was thinking about Ed Watkins, a tutor at the local college of further education who'd been reluctant to admit him to a crash course of German, and who'd repeatedly questioned him about his motivation. He could hear Ed's peremptory high pitched speech pattern ringing in his ears.

'You will find it difficult at your age, Mr Pringle, to absorb our six week course.'

'I doubt it,' replied Andrew firmly. 'I already have a smattering, but I need more than that, and I'm quite determined to spend every minute of every day until I'm fluent.'

Ed Watkins looked at the set jaw of the man sitting in front of him.

'You're determined, Mr Pringle, I'll say that for you, but what does a man of nearly seventy want with fluent German? It is an expensive course, mostly taken up by business people?'

'If you're asking me whether, as a pensioner, I can afford £550, the answer is, yes.'

'Very well, Mr Pringle, I'll put you in the picture. We keep the classes to a maximum of six. That way each student receives a considerable amount of personal tuition. We are equipped with all the latest language laboratory paraphernalia. There is one vacancy on the course which commences next week, and when you have signed...'

Andrew interrupted, 'I'll be there.' Ed Watkins, he thought, would never in a thousand years have guessed why he needed the crash course in German.

Sleep didn't come easily. It had nothing to do with being in a strange bed, but everything to do with what was on his mind. Andrew gave up and as he walked round the Botanic Gardens at 6 o' clock in the morning he was not surprised to find himself alone. A strange way, he thought, to spend my seventieth birthday. Today there'll be no card from Emily, which she'd always insisted on posting no matter how much he'd protested. And no card from Joyce. He tried not to think about his daughter. Thinking about her made him feel uneasy, guilty, but now was not the time for introspection. It was while he was concentrating on the gyrations of the fish in the lake that he suddenly realised he'd not thought about how he was going to kill the German pilot, then with extraordinary clarity, as he rejected poison, strangulation or a knife in the back, he saw the scene unfold before him. How simple it had all become. With a gun, of course. Fate, in the form of Francis Dadswell had played straight into his hands. He'd find this man, check up on his daily routines, choose a place off the beaten track, and kill him face to face. He'd like to tell him why he was being executed but there might not be time for that.

The staff car, Francis had said, would pick him up at 0900 hours. With luck he'd manage two hours practice. That should be enough. Shooting should be like cycling or swimming, an aptitude acquired that one never really loses. All he needed was a little practice. He wandered slowly back to the hotel. Yes, he'd enjoy his breakfast.

Corporal Carey pulled up in front of the hotel and hooted. He wasn't sure whether the elderly man with a shock of grey hair, who seemed to be day-dreaming, was his passenger. Andrew came to, gave him a nod, and climbed in beside him.

'Good morning, sir.'

'Morning, Corporal. It's all right is it, sitting in the front, means I can see more?'

'Naow skin orf my nose, sir. Group Captain said you'd like to take a quick shifty at the Stadium where the army's based, so I'd better put my foot down,' said the Corporal as he crept back into a solid stream of traffic, dexterously manoeuvring the car into Lepsius Strasse.

'Do you enjoy living in Berlin, Corporal?'

'Yes, sir. The best posting I've 'ad for years, and my last.'

'Why's that?'

'I've completed my twenty two years.'

'Can't you sign on for another stretch?'

'Naow, not now. Could 'ave done once, but now now, not since the Cold War ended. Anyway my wife 'as 'ad enough. She wants to go 'ome.'

'That's London, is it?'

'Naow, she's a country girl. 'Er father farms in Devon, but I'm not one for the open spaces,' he said turning into Schildhorn Strasse.

'So what will you do?'

'Live in Devon, probably, but I'm a car man myself, 'I'll be much 'appier in a garage than on a farm cleaning out pig sties.'

'Useful with your hands, eh?'

'You could say that, but I guess we'll end up in Exeter, not too near the in-laws, and not too far.'

Andrew laughed. 'It seems to me, my friend, you've got it all mapped out.'

''Ave to, sir. Always 'ave to be one step ahead of the missus.' Corporal Carey took a sideways look at his passenger. 'You're a good shot, are you, sir?'

'I've no idea. Why do you ask?'

'Groupie said to drop you at the range, so I thought you might be doing a little target practice.'

'Yes, I am. As a matter of fact it will be the first time I've handled fire-arms since the war. I've had a go on fairgrounds with those instruments they laughingly call rifles, always hopelessly inaccurate and never favouring the marksman, but I am looking forward to having a go with the real mccoy. It could provide me with a rewarding hobby.'

'Not my idea of a hobby, sir. I like something a bit more active.'

'If,' said Andrew nonchantly, 'if I decided to take up the sport seriously where in Berlin could I purchase a gun, and would I need a licence?'

'You can buy anything, guv, in Berlin if you've got the lolly, but the Germans 'ave been tightning up on the sale of fire-arms, trying to put a stop to all these terrorist activities.'

'So you think it would be difficult?'

'I'd wait until you get back to England, sir, much easier. Join a club, get a licence, like my brother 'as done.

Leaving the slow traffic on the Schildhorn Strasse, Corporal Carey slid into the faster traffic on the ring road to Halensee.

'What's that impressive building on the left adjacent to the tower?'

'It's the International Congress Centre, and the tower is the Funkturm, the radio tower. All them buildings you see round it are used for exhibitions. You should climb up the tower, sir, there's one 'ell of a view from the top. You can see the Charlottenburg Palace which 'ouses several museums, but my wife prefers to be on the ground, loves the gardens she does. You a gardener, sir?'

'I was,' said Andrew softly.

'From the top,' said the Corporal not waiting for an answer, 'you can also see the Olympic Stadium which looks bloody magnificent from a distance, and the column which stands in the Theodor-Heuss-Platz. On the top there's one of them everlasting flames.'

'What's that in aid of?'

'Justice, liberty, and peace, so I'm told.'

Justice, thought Andrew bitterly. That's what this is all about.'

'Do you want to 'op out, sir?' asked Corporal Carey as they approached the entrance to the Olympic Stadium. 'I could meet you on the other side of the arena.'

'Thanks, Corporal, I'll do that.'

Andrew walked towards the centre of the stadium and stood for a time hearing the roar of the crowd as they spurred on the competitors. He shook himself. It was a strangely eerie place, a crumbling, disintegrating concrete edifice which would never again house an international event. A place where Hitler's arrogant Nazi Youth Corps had paraded, flaunting their fitness and invincibility; a place where hundreds of young blond machen provided their Führer with carefully orchestrated displays of physical fitness, all totally regimented, precise, perfect but lacking natural exuberance.

His chauffeur was waiting in the shadow of the great stands.

'Impressive, Corporal.'

'Wait until you see Gatow, that's something else.!'

Less than half an hour later they drove through a magnificent archway, round a chicane, past imposing buildings, grand but tasteless, decorated with bas relief medallions and sculptured faces. More like a half finished cathedral then RAF HQ.

'Everything that 'appens 'ere, sir, can be seen by the Russians. I used to wave to them sometimes and shout '*allo Ivan* but they never waved back. See those buildings over there? Well Group Captain 'as the best 'ouse, it's like a bloomin palace.'

'Yes, I know, Corporal.'

A guard on duty outside the range took a good look at him as he climbed out of the car. Yes, the six-foot stranger with the mass of unruly grey hair matched the Group's description. Andrew stood silently watching Francis Dadswell, who was in a kneeling position, firing at a small target. It was impossible to see the results. Time, he thought, I did something about my distance vision. A sergeant marched over to the Group Captain, waited until he'd emtied his magazine then told him that his visitor had arrived.

'Good morning, Andrew, you ready for the fray?' asked \Dadswell.

'As ready as I'll ever be, but the target needs to be a great deal nearer. I can't even see what you've scored.'

'Two bulls, and eight inners. Not good enough. There's no wind today. All those shots should have been spot on. However, you are here to enjoy yourself. What do you fancy? 3.03's, 2.2's, revolvers, or the latest Russian jobs?'

'Revolvers, I think, Francis. For one thing the target will be a lot closer. You must allow for my advanced age.'

'I didn't make allowances when we played tennis. You kept me on my toes. But, if you want to have a go with revolvers, Sergeant Fletcher is your man. He's a born instructor, no one better. Sergeant!' he yelled.

A heavily built man looking every inch an ex-boxer appeared from the shadows. 'Sir?'

'Sergeant, Mr Pringle has decided to try his luck with revolvers. Unlock the store, will you, and let him take his pick. Give him enough ammo because I guarantee he'll not be anywhere near the target to start with.'

'Such encouragement,' laughed Andrew.

Sergeant Fletcher unlocked both the store and a case containing revolvers of all shapes and sizes. Andrew looked at them bewildered.

'You'd better advise me, Sergeant.'

'It's a question of what you fancy, sir. The weight could be important.'

'It's 45 years since I last handled a gun, so I guess it would be sensible for starters to begin with something small. A sort of everyday revolver, not one of those up to date fire-arms one sees on the box, a sort of cross between a rifle and a revolver, and too large for comfort.'

'Something small,' repeated the sergeant, 'something that Philip Marlowe or James Bond could have hidden up their trouser legs?' He looked at Andrew with a knowing grin on his face. He knew all about the hidden fantasies in which men both young and old indulged when they had their finger on the trigger.

'Well how about trying this Smith and Wesson, Model 669.? It holds a 12-shot box magazine in the butt, and has a short recoil. A nice comfortable gun.

'Yes, why not!'

'We have a range discipline, sir. Load the magazine off the range, take it to the butts and then slot it in.'

With his first eight shots he totally missed the target. He reloaded slowly.

'You need to use both hands, sir, and stand with your feet apart.'

'Sergeant Fletcher is quite right, Andrew, methods have totally changed since the war.'

With both hands on the gun and his feet apart he took careful aim, managing to get two shots on target.

'You'll have to be faster than that, my friend. The enemy would have finished you off by now.'

'Oh, I don't think so, Francis,' said Andrew quietly. 'My enemy won't be armed.'

'Your enemy, Andrew?'

Andrew realising his blunder laughed it off. 'Yes, time is my enemy.'

'Doesn't that apply to all of us?'

A hundred rounds and an hour later Andrew felt on top of the world. He'd cracked it. He'd mastered the lethal machine, a small revolver which he could slip into his inner pocket. If, as he now knew, he could hit the target nine times out of ten at a range of fifteen yards he was going to have no difficulty face to face. The only problem left was how to obtain a revolver, but there'd be a way, he'd find a way. He was a great believer in positive thinking.

Lunch in the Officers' Mess was a leisurely affair. No hostilities to concern them now, only a war of nerves with the IRA, but that wasn't troubling any of the men round this table. Now was the time to satisfy his curiosity about some aspects of life in Berlin.

'Francis, can you or any of your colleagues explain why Berlin, which has been cut off from the rest of West Germany for so long, shows no sign of suffering from the situation. The entire city seems so affluent. And why, if you don't mind me asking, is the RAF so pampered?'

Some of the young officers looked amused, but most of the men resented the word 'pampered'.

'It's quite simple, Andrew. From the moment the wall was erected the Federal Government poured endless resources into

West Berlin creating a city which, for the past three decades, has vied with Paris and London. Its citizens have not been denied. Every luxury here, food in plenty, nightclubs, opera, theatre, sports facilities of every kind, a cleanliness absent in London, and a city as fashionable as Paris. As for your second question the armed forces have never been pampered. We've quietly got on with the job, and have always been ready for any emergency. If you're thinking of the way our wives have been catered for, that's another question. The ladies, from my wife down to the aircraftmen's wives have all been given allowances to pay for help in the home. Their free time has been more usefully spent in acquiring other skills. There have been classes here in everything you can imagine from upholstery to business studies. On top of that they have social get-togethers, entertainment, sport, and excellent schooling for the kids. A few may want to return to England, but the majority realise they've never had it so good. Now the Cold War is coming to an end I guess everything for the Berliner will change, and Federal largesse will be more evenly spread'

'This book that you're writing Mr Pringle, does it cover the entire war or merely the exploits of Bomber Command.'

'Merely!' barked Andrew before he could stop himself is not a word I'd ever use in conjunction with Bomber Command.'

Dadswell looked surprised but Wing Commander Harvey apologised immediately. 'Forgive me, sir, for my misuse of the English language. I'm a twit.'

Andrew laughed. 'My fault. I have this thing, you see about the horrendous way in which Bomber Command was treated at the end of the war.

Now, if you'll excuse me, I have an appointment, and regretfully, Andrew, I'll have to miss my confrontation with Verdi on Friday night. A diplomatic assignment has cropped up. You'll find Corporal Carey standing by to take you back to the hotel.

'Andrew was angry. The two expensive tickets he was carrying in his wallet had cost him 150 marks. Tickets he'd bought to repay the Group Captain's hospitality.

'I don't need the car, Francis. What I need is fresh air. I am going to take the lift to the top of the Funkturm, or *Little Eiffel,* as they call it, and after that enjoy the peace of the Charlottenburg Gardens. Francis Dadswell got the message.

Two days later Andrew was in Freiburg, capital of the Black Forest, which he found unbelievably beautiful. Not the place to waste time pouring over musty smelling reports of another life nearly half a century away, but the place where one's spirit needs to be free. Emily would have loved the spectacular cathedral with its soaring lacework steeple set against a background of impressive mountains. The interior was breathtaking, mercifully undamaged during the war, with its man made miracles, wood carvings, paintings, stained glass windows, tapestries, a medieval celebration for all to see.

Sightseeing was not Andrew's intent, but the temptation had been too great, and after a snack lunch he set about trying to find a hotel, which was far from easy in a city full of holiday makers. At long last he managed to track down a room at the *Stephanie* in Poststrasse, a quiet hotel with no restaurant. He signed in, left his luggage and walked to the Milititärgeschichtliches Forschungsamt.

The hotel receptionist had given him clear instructions. "The Military building is opposite Hittlages, an up market clothing store," she had said. "You can't miss it! It's a four-storey building with expensive boutiques and restaurants on the ground floor. The military use the top three floors, and to reach them you need to make your way to the centre of the ground floor where there is an open space covered by a glass pyramid. There you will find a passage which leads to the entrance hall of the MGFA, that's what they call the Militargeschichtliches Forschungsamt, such a mouthful, isn't it?"

Andrew following her instructions to the letter stepped into a small lift which took him up to the first floor. A middle aged man in Reception with tired blue eyes and greying hair asked the English visitor to take a seat while he tracked down Doctor Erlbach. 'The Brigadier General,' he confided, 'could be anywhere in this rabbit warren of a building.'

Browsing through the coffee table literature Andrew was totally engrossed in a slender volume on the *Messerschmidt 109* when a quiet voice broke his train of thought.

'Herr Pringle, greetings and apologies for keeping you waiting. I have, of course, been expecting you.'

Andrew was totally unprepared for the man with warm brown eyes, a short man in his early fifties, not wearing uniform, every inch a scholar, with wispy hair curling round his collar. He'd been expecting Brigadier Erlbach to have the bearing of a military man, short hair, clipped speech and who, decades earlier, would have clicked his heels and said "Heil Hitler." I'm stupid, he thought, as he shook hands with Doctor Brigadier Erlbach. It's not yesterday, it's today.

They made their way, via a narrow staircase, to Doctor Erlbach's office on the second floor. A room, which reflected the character of the man, with excellent reproductions of Dürer gracing the walls, and on the desk surrounded by paper, a small metal sculpture of a head by Paolozzi. The Brigadier served coffee from an ever ready dispenser on a table in a corner of the room. 'It's black, I'm afraid, Herr Pringle. Will that suit you?'

'Yes thank you.'

'Coffee is my life force. I don't bother to stop for lunch, not enough hours in the day for that. Do have a comfortable seat.'

Andrew sat on the only easy chair while Doctor Erlbach rooted around under the mountain of papers on his desk.

'Ah, here we are. The letter from Group Captain Dadswell,' he announced triumphantly. My desk may look a mess, Herr Pringle, but I know where everything is, and my secretary is never allowed to touch a single paper, not while I'm working on my next monograph.'

'May I ask what it's about?'

'Yes, of course. The subject, though fascinating, may hold no interest for modernists. I'm writing about the development of the tank in a historical context, not its place in modern warfare, although I do believe that in another twenty years the age of the tank will be over. An idea that may not appeal to many of my colleagues.'

He scanned the letter in front of him. 'Francis Dadswell has unusually broad interests, not least his deep interest in Wagnerian opera. It's a pity we don't meet more often. I see, from his brief note, that you're writing a book about the Royal Air Force and would like to do some cross referencing in the

Luftwaffe Annals which cover the 1939-45 war. There is no problem, my friend, it is easily arranged.'

'Thank you, that is most kind.' Here, dammit, thought Andrew, is another man I don't like taking for a ride, but there's no other way to obtain the information I need. There was a sharp tap on the door.

'Come in Colonel,' shouted Doctor Erlbach. 'Herr Pringle I'd like you to meet Doctor Fassbinder who is the Colonel in charge of Education and Information.'

Andrew looked at the two men in amazement.

'What's the matter, Herr Pringle?'

'I'd never thought of military personnel being so...so informed.   Do you all have doctorates?'

Dr Fassbinder smiled as he shook the Englishman's hand. 'You have to be educated in this place, it's rather like a superior university, and yes, we do all have degrees. There are, roughly speaking, fifty scholars aged between 27 and 65 working here in the MGFA, half military, and half civilian including, of course, Brigadier Erlbach who is our Amtschef, or Chief as you say in English.'

'The Brigadier laughed. 'Your Chief would now like you to take care of Herr Pringle. Make sure he has everything he requires, including a Reader's Ticket. One thing you won't have to do Doctor Fassbinder is translate because Herr Pringle speaks German like a native.'

Andrew followed Doctor Fassbinder along narrow corridors and up stairs to the third floor.

'My office is adjacent to the library, Herr Pringle. If you need further help during your research here please don't hesitate to ask me. That's what I'm here for. This is the library,' he said as he opened the door to a room covered in books from floor to ceiling. 'There are roughly 60,000 books all on general and military history. The majority of scholars are conducting research into the history of the Second World War, or the history of NATO and the Western Union.'

Andrew looked round the room at the men and women sitting at the desks reading. All engrossed in a task they enjoyed. He wasn't here to enjoy himself; he wanted to get through the reading as fast as possible and be off and doing. It's as well, he thought, that Doctor Fassbinder can't mind read.

'Let's go and sit in my office, Herr Pringle. It's adjacent to the library, but a little more comfortable.'

Through the window Andrew could see the Cathedral and thought once again about Emily, and how she would have loved Freiburg. But Freiburg was a city Emily would adamantly have refused to visit. She wouldn't have approved of his research, she'd always hated the idea of retribution. It's a pity, Emily, I've had to wait so long. Wait until you'd gone. No words, no looks, no emotions, no involvement to stop me now.

'Perhaps,' said Doctor Fassbinder quietly, 'you could tell me a little more about the book you are writing, and how we can help?'

'It's about the RAF and covers Bomber Command's exploits during the hostilities from 1939 to 1945.' He lied convincingly. It became easier every time he said it. In fact, why not write a book about the RAF, he could certainly draw on his own experiences and write descriptively about the war from a pilot's viewpoint? But that was wishful thinking. When he'd finished what he'd set out to do there would be no more time for him, and what did he want time for? His life had almost come full circle. Only one more objective before he made his exit from this mortal coil.

'The exploits of Bomber Command would make interesting reading,' said Doctor Fassbinder politely, thinking the while of Hamburg and Dresden, 'but how can we help?'

'It's all been fairly straight forward until now, but 1945 has created problems. I need more corroborative evidence which I'm not able to pick up in our Public Record Office at Kew.'

'I see. January to May, 1945. Four and a half months. That's a lot of reading to cover, Herr Pringle. Could take you quite a time to go through all the Commands; Coastal, Fighter, Bomber, Training and Maintenance. All fully documented in a most detailed way, but we'd need precise instruction because no documents or archive are held in this building.'

'What!' Andrew almost leapt out of his seat. 'But....but Dadswell said everything would be to hand.'

'Almost to hand, but all archival material used for research has to be requested one day and is delivered the following day by a messenger from the Bundesarchiv-Militararchiv.' Doctor Fassbinder looked at the bewildered man in front of him. Hadn't he done research before? Didn't he know it was the same at the British Museum? The last time he'd been there himself he'd put in a chit for one book and had to wait two hours for it to be brought to him.

'There is no cause for concern, Herr Pringle. The Bundesarchiv a department of the German Federal Archives is also in Freiburg, and situated in Wiesenthalstrasse. It comes under the jurisdiciton of the Ministry of the Interior. Naturally we in the MGFA enjoy a close working relationship with the Bundesarchiv, and despite the fact that we are a military establishment freedom of research is guaranteed by law in

West Germany, so all you have to do is order what you require today, and it will arrive tomorrow.'

Andrew wondered whether, like the Record Office at Kew, they too made use of embargoes, which lasted thirty years, sometimes more, but decided at this point it would not be politic to ask.

'What exactly are you looking for, Herr Pringle?'

Andrew decided truth would be better than fiction. 'Having read a broad history of the Luftwaffe in the Staatsbibliothek I now need to check up on German Fighter Command operations during 1945, and tie them in with events in Britain.'

'Can you be a bit more specific, Herr Pringle?'

'I'll try. The most difficult period to cover has been March and April 1945. For instance very little is known in England about *Operation Giselle*. In fact, when I was researching at Kew in 1984 I couldn't find a single reference to the operation. It may be there now, of course.'

'Ah,' said Doctor Fassbinder smiling happily for the first time. 'That was one of our success stories. Let me see what my computer throws up.'

Andrew couldn't wait to see. He moved round the desk and peered over Doctor Fassbinder's shoulder, but at that distance it was difficult to see clearly. He really must get his eyes tested. He put his reading glasses on and moved closer to the screen until his head was almost blocking the Doctor's view.

'There you are, Herr Pringle. *Unternehmen Gisela*. We're not short of information on that little operation. We even have an English Air Research Publication by Simon Parry, *English Intruders Over Britain*. And, here's another,' he said excitedly, '*Battle Over the Reich* by Alfred Price. In fact, I believe there's a copy of that in the library. It's all here, Herr Pringle.'

'It is, isn't it,' said Andrew in a whisper.

'Would you like me to indent for everything that's on the screen and have it sent over tomorrow?'

'Yes, please do. I'd like to get started as soon as possible.'

'In the meantime you could take a look at *Battle Over the Reich*. You should find it with the English publications at the far end of the library. Probably in a red file.'

Andrew wasted no time. It took him less than five minutes to find the red file which protected the slender publication. His hand shook as he took it off the shelf. Suddenly he felt dizzy, the room became deathly quiet, he could feel his heart beat, could have sworn it was beating faster. Closing his eyes, he tried to forget the tightness in his chest, the floating sensation in his head and the fact that his knees felt ten times their normal size.

'Ist Ihnen nicht gut, Herr Pringle?'

'Nein, nein danke,' he managed to utter. 'Vielleicht kann ich hier einen Moment sitzen.' The stranger helped him to the nearest desk where he sat for some moments, trembling and wondering why success should have affected him in such an unlikely manner.

He took a deep breath, steadied himself, and settled down to read. What he read was beyond the realms of anything he'd imagined. Why had he thought that only a single squadron of Junkers 88's had infiltrated returning formations of Bombers? Was that what they'd been led to believe? Or was it what they'd dreamt up? Or was it the bloody Air Ministry doing a cover-up? The truth, he thought, closing his eyes and putting his head in his hands, is very different.

The young officer at the next table, who was writing a treatise on the Western Alliance, kept an eye on the grey haired Englishman who seemed to be suffering. Should he alert Dr Fassbinder, in case the old man had a heart attack? Or should he leave well alone? I'd look stupid, he thought, if it's only the onset of Summer flu. Much better not to get involved. He put his head down and tried to concentrate.

Andrew opened his eyes and re-read a graphic description of *Operation Giselle* the last desperate onslaught by the Luftwaffe on English airfields. Two large waves of Heinkel 219's and Junkers 88's had swept over the North Sea with orders to attack 27 airfields in Norfolk, Suffolk, Yorkshire and Lincolnshire with cannon, machine gun and bombs. 48 aircraft came under attack of which 22 were shot down and 8 planes suffered damage. The intruders also attacked the poor rookies on training flights. On the night of March 3rd/4th, 1945 the Germans only lost 6 aircraft. It was an operation never to be repeated. Damnation! The date is wrong. Pete was killed in the early hours of April 3rd. There was no wave of German fighters. One was enough. Just one.

It's taken me 45 years to get this far and the damned facts don't fit. From his wallet he surreptiously removed a crumpled newspaper cutting, and stared at the image of nine German airmen who were reunited at Hendon, so the article said, with a Junkers 88. It also mentioned *Intruders Over Britain* written by Simon Parry and published in 1987. Perhaps he should have short circuited his research and made contact with Mr Parry? No, that would have been crass stupidity. He had to go it alone. It was his problem. There had to be ways of discovering the identity ofthe lone German pilot who flew over Waddington in the early hours of April 3rd. Fighter Command Operations for April should, with luck, give him a lead, but it meant waiting, waiting until the following morning. 45 years of his life had been spent waiting, but he knew the next twenty four hours would seem endless.

He glanced at the young man at the next table who was busy writing, using a thick pad and pencil. That's something he'd forgotten, but it could be remedied. After all he had an afternoon and evening to kill. After lunch he'd acquire a brief case, pad and pencils because, according to notices prominently displayed, pens were verbotem in the library, and later he'd walk, get some of this aggro out of his system. Francis Dadswell had given him a short list of MUSTS; top of the list was a walk round Rathaus Square where the City Hall is situated. A magnificent and unusual building formed by joining two 16th century Patrician houses, both complete with Renaissance gables and oriels. The southern one, *The Maiden and Unicorn*, Francis had said, was built in 1545.

He was right the square was beautiful. He purchased the brief case, pad and pencils and then returned to the hotel for a bath, before making tracks towards the second MUST on his list. The Red Bear or the *Zum Roten Bären* in Oberlinden Square, once a medieval burgher house, and now one of the oldest inns in Germany. It still provides Black Forest specialities in a restaurant where the atmosphere takes one straight back to the Middle Ages. As he sat at a small table drinking a fine Kabinett, and sampling local trout Andrew mused on the kindness and hospitality of the Germans he'd met, and their ability to speak English never expecting him to reply in German. For them, first the shock, and then the pleasure at hearing him speak their own language, and speak it well, was all too evident, but nothing, absolutely nothing would divert him from his purpose.

The following morning he arose to a grey overcast miserable day. From his bedroom window he looked down on bedraggled tourists who were going to walk whatever the weather. That's what they'd come for. The constant drizzle did nothing to dampen Andrew's spirits. He arrived in the library at the very moment Leutnant Lösemann, Dr Fassbinder's assistant, placed a pile of documents and files on the table in the corner where the English publications were kept. The young man smiled at him. 'This little lot will keep you out of mischief Herr Pringle.'

'Ah, young man, my mischief is ordained. Nothing can stop me now.'

Leutnant Lösemann looked at him in astonishment. Andrew laughed out loud causing the young man to place his fingers on his lips to indicate silence.

'Yes,' whispered Andrew, 'I'll keep it quiet.'

Andrew opened his brief case which he'd bought, not for his note pad and pencils, but as a container for something he had yet to purchase. He must look like a scholar, act like a scholar, and not draw attention to himself. Quietly and methodically he sorted through the documents extracting only those that referred to March and April 1945. Ah, here was an interesting paper, attached to the front of the March records. Written in 1941, and unsigned. Here the germ of an idea was born. The writer proposed that a squadron of Junkers 88 nightfighters should trail RAF bombers back to base. Theorising too about the safety of the German planes, and suggesting that they'd be relatively safe because the British anti-aircraft defences would hesitate to fire for fear of hitting their own aircraft. *Attack the bombers as they land, attack them when they are most vulnerable* said the writer. An idea which, fortunately, had been left to moulder until desperate measures were needed.

Details of Fighter Command's planning and conduct were quite clear, but only on a broad basis. There was no reference to an attack carried out in the early hours of April 3rd. There was nothing for it but to plod painstakingly through the daily records of every fighter base. The Operation Record Books of each squadron would contain daily and monthly summaries. He'd also expect to find details of aircraft, crew, weapons, and casualties. That's how they'd done it in the RAF.

Operation Giselle, he had to admit had been master minded by a genius. If similar attacks had been repeatedly carried out in 1941 and 1942 Hitler could have invaded England with ease. Instead he broke faith with his Russian ally, diverted his forces to the Eastern Front, and paid the price.

It was a fruitless morning. Interesting for a historian, but it held little interest for a would-be assassin. Andrew cast his mind back to the British raid on Rotterdam. He knew exactly how the reports he and his crew had given at the de-briefing read, right from the moment they left Waddington, to the moment they returned to base. The raid had been detailed and difficult. Orders to hit one particular building. No damage to the civilian population. Rotterdam wasn't too far, only seven hours cooped up in the crate, but on that sortie they were heavily protected by Beaufighters equipped with a secret weapon code named *Serrate*. All the men flying on the mission were unaware that on the 9th May, 1943, a Junkers 88 nightfighter had landed undamaged and intact on Dyce Airfield near Aberdeen. This extraordinary arrival was no accident. It was expected. There was no more bizarre sight in wartime than to see a German fighter being heavily escorted by a squadron of Spitfires. The Spitfire pilots believed the Germans had defected. They had no knowledge of the radar equipment they were bringing with them. *Lichtenstein* was a priceless gift which proved invaluable to British scientists. When the boffins had finished their tests they were able to produce a homing device using radar pulses which enabled RAF fighters to locate German planes, and destroy them with an accuracy never known before.

The actual Junkers 88, which Andrew had seen many times displayed in the RAF Museum at Hendon was also pictured on the scrappy newspaper cutting he was carrying in his wallet. He took it out and read, for the umpteenth time, the names of nine German airmen. Could one of them be the man he was seeking? They were all exploring the inside of a Junkers for the first time in 40 years, the Junkers that had delivered such precious secrets. No one of Andrew's age will ever know who delivered this invaluable aircraft. The files held in the Public Record Office at Kew remain closed until 2043, a century after the event.

The Rotterdam raid had been successful. They'd arrived on the scene 15 minutes after the Pathfinders had dropped *Window* their chaos causing confetti, which had totally botched up the enemy's radar. After the confetti they dropped red and green flares clearly marking the aiming point. That night over Rotterdam the two squadrons from Waddington had hit the Headquarters of the Gestapo with devastating accuracy. Photographs after the raid showed a direct hit.

On their way back to base Squadron Leader Timmings, no longer worrying about air silence came over the waves chortling like a schoolboy who had just scored his first hundred. "We've done it lads, out with the coffee, and the sandwiches and on with the motley." In each craft thermos caps were unscrewed and ersatz coffee imbibed as though it were vintage champagne. Unlucky to drink it on the way out---a celebratory drink for when the job was done. Andrew wondered how that strange tradition had evolved.

By half past two on the morning of April 3rd they were approaching their base preparatory to landing. Pete was in the second Lancaster, Andrew in the fifth. Flares clearly visible marked the runway. The first plane landed and was taxying down the runway when it was attacked, and in seconds it became a ball of fire. A shot searing the wings which contained the fuel tanks was all it needed. The second Lancaster, with its undercarriage fully down was approaching the runway when it too was attacked and exploded like a thunder bolt in mid air.

'Christ! Pete's caught it skipper.' Nobby's voice came clearly over the intercom, and at the same time the Control Tower gave them orders to disperse. An order he ignored until common sense came to his aid.

Focus your attention, he told himself, get back to your reading, find which station carried out an attack on the night Pete and his crew were incinerated.

Andrew found concentration difficult and the work incredibly tiring. Scholars, he decided, didn't enjoy the cushy life he always imagined. His feet were frozen, his eyes tired, and his limbs stiff. Another frustrating day spent pouring over meticulously produced records which had yielded nothing. Hour after hour after hour, with nothing to show for it. Why was it so difficult to keep his mind on the job? If by the end of the afternoon he'd made no headway he would ask Leftenant Lösemann for assistance.

He was drowsy, almost asleep, as he scanned the April records for an airfield, not far from Nijmegen on the German-Dutch border. 'Eureka', he yelled triumphantly, and hastily put his head down as the other readers gazed at the elderly man who'd echoed, more loudly than necessary, a word which Archimedes, the most celebrated of Greek mathematicians, had used 200 years before Christ. Andrew was breathing heavily. Take it easy, take it easy, he told himself. There were the words dancing in front of his eyes, a few words written 45 years ago. Two aircraft, G12 and G13, ordered to stand-by, to be on the alert. German Intelligence had informed Fighter Command that two squadrons of Lancasters had left a Lincolnshire airfield and were heading across the North Sea in the direction of Rotterdam. G12 was ordered to infiltrate the first squadron as it returned to base, and G13 the second. Not part of *Operation Giselle* thought Andrew. This was a one off.

The pilots of G12 and G13 were not named. What he needed now was a sight of the debriefing carried out after the attacks. He stood up trying not to look excited or too keen. Doctor Fassbinder had gone, only Lösemann remained. Andrew moved slowly towards the office. His feet were excruciatingly painful as the blood began to circulate. The door was open. Lösemann was busy on the computer transmitting readers' requests for papers needed in the morning.

'Come in, Herr Pringle. What is the problem, and how can I help?'

'Apologies, Lieutenant for leaving my order so late but, as I plan to leave Freiburg tomorrow, I haven't much time.'

'What do you need?'

'Not too much.'

Lösemann thought about his girl friend who ran a boutique on the ground floor and would be waiting for him.

'I'd like to read through the debriefing Combat Reports made at the Fighter Command base at Nijmegen on the night of April 2nd, 1945.'

'If that's all you need, Herr Pringle, I can run it off on the computer.'

'You can!'

The Englishman looked so amazed, and then so pleased that LÖsemann, despite wanting to get off duty, hammered away at the computer until information came up on the screen, He ran off a copy and handed it to Andrew.

'Sit down, Herr Pringle, make sure it's exactly what you want.'

Leutnant Lösemann carried on typing. Not many more requests. A few more minutes and he'd be away on time.

Andrew sat not daring to move a muscle. It was all there. G12 was flown by OberLeutnant Marx who successfully infiltrated the first squadron of Lancasters. Andrew remembered the men in the first squadron. They all spoke another language, they all nursed a deep seated hatred for the oppressors who'd torn their country apart. They were Poles. As Oberleutnant Marx neared the English coast his Junkers developed engine trouble, and he managed to return safely to base. So much for G12. Now for G13, flown by Oberleutnant Helmut Schmidt, who managed in thick cloud, to tuck himself into the centre of a squadron of Lancasters. His report made it clear that he'd concentrated on attacking three planes as they landed. The first and second were totally destroyed and the third crash landed. In the Combat Report Schmidt was adamant about the direct hits, but not too sure which airfield because he'd beat a hasty retreat. Somewhere over Lincolnshire was his guess. I can tell you which airfield, you bastard, thought Andrew. He was nearly there. All he needed now was Schmidt's address, and if he thought his prayer would be answered he'd willingly get down on his knees to Leutnant Lösemann and plead.

The German could feel Herr Pringle's eyes on him.

'Leutnant Lösemann,' said Andrew softly, 'I wonder, and I know this is asking a bit much at the end of the day, but can you extract details from Fighter Command's Personnel Records, even if they go back to 1945?'

'Yes,' said the German grudgingly, 'yes, I can. What is it you want?'

'I'd like to write an article about one of these pilots. A certain Helmut Schmidt who was based at Nijmegen.'

'There's no guarantee, Herr Pringle, that you'll be able to track him down. Addresses and telephone numbers haven't been updated.'

'Oh, that's a bit of a facer.' The Englishman looked crushed.

Why, wondered the young German Officer, was one particular pilot so important? 'Don't worry, sir, I'll do what I can now, see what comes up.'

It was five minutes past the hour when Lösemann handed Andrew a print-out.

'That's all we have, if it's of any use.'

Andrew controlled himself. Took care not to grab the sheet of paper. Smiled at the German before taking it, and shook his hand.

'Thank you, you've been most patient and helpful. I'll only be in for a brief period tomorrow morning, to make sure I have everything I need.'

Lösemann cut short the goodbye and the thanks. 'If you'll excuse me, Herr Pringle, I have an appointment, but there's no need for you to hurry. Take your time. You've another half hour before the library closes.' The young officer turned off the computer, locked the office and ran. Helga never liked to be kept waiting.

LÖsemann was right.There'd been no update on the wartime addresses.

Helmut Schmidt was a popular name. There were five based at Nijmegen. The first one had been a navigator, the second a gunner, the third a wireless operator, and the fourth and fifth both pilots. He was lucky. There were notes against all the men listed. The first of the pilots was stationed in Austria. *Wounded when attacking HMS Illustrious in the Mediterranean. Arm amputated and given a desk job.* So much for number one. Let's see if I have more luck with number two. *Helmut Schmidt based Station BGH in Denmark where he flew Messerschmidt 109's then transferred to Nijmegen.*

8 successful missions. Awarded the Iron Cross. Studied law when off duty in order to enter the Landrat's Office in Wittlich at the end of hostilities.

Come on, come on, all I want now, you bastard, is your address. He hit the table with his fist. Damn! Damn! Damn! Nothing.

Andrew sat motionless for some time before he made up his mind. He knew what he had to do.

SIX

Speed was essential, decided the Inspector. Driving to Berlin would take too long. Flying was the answer. He would fly and Joyce could drive **the car** back to Oxford. When they arrived back in Limoges after their visit to Oradour, he encouraged Joyce to continue pottering round the souvenir shops, while he settled down in their hotel bedroom to make three phone calls. P & O, Air France, and Group Captain Dadswell. Yes, P & O had space on the following day, Wednesday; yes, a seat was available on the early morning flight, on Thursday, from Paris to Berlin; no, was an exasperated contumacious Captain's initial reaction, but finally, when he'd simmered down, gave way. 'Ten minutes, Inspector, ten minutes on Thursday morning at 11.30.'

Joyce was shaken by the decision to end their few days holiday so abruptly. She couldn't fathom why it was necessary to dash off to Berlin on a sudden whim. Another couple of days meandering through France would make little difference to their search. Why didn't he return to England with her where he could just as easily fly from Heathrow? She slept badly that night realising for the first time the truth of Sergeant Fielding's incautious remark when he'd called at the house two months previously. "Oh, he's a law unto himself, Mrs Venning. Does what he wants, when he wants, puts everyone's nose out of joint, but he gets things done." She found herself sympathising, for the first time, with Rhoda, Julian's ex, who'd left a short sharp note on the kitchen table for him. *Stay married to your job, boyo. You've no time in your life for people.* How any mother could leave her child was totally incomprehensible, but she was beginning to understand why Rhoda had done a bunk. Work before family. Would it always be that way?

Madame, who provided them with an early breakfast, couldn't help noticing that they too had changed since their visit to the *Village of the Martyrs*. What on earth was there at Oradour that created such unhappiness and disquiet for two English women who'd not lost their own families during the massacre? First Emily Pringle, five years earlier, and now her daughter, both sitting sJulian faced at breakfast, both ignoring their husbands.

'Le Havre,' said Venning as they drove along the N147, 'will take us about seven or eight hours. We should be there about 4 o'clock, give us plenty of time to take a look at the town which has an impressive square.'

'How do you know?'

'I attended a two-day conference there about five years ago at the Maison de la Culture. The conference bored the pants off me, but it was useful for its contacts. I can't complain, though, because my seat at dinner gave me a ringside view of flowers and fountains in a magnificent square. You'll love it. French planning at its best, all designed and built since the war.'

Joyce lapsed into silence thinking how little she knew about her husband, about his other life which she could never penetrate, and how little she had shared with him about her own background, and her struggle to find work away from home. She was in her early twenties before she escaped and found work as an assistant matron in a minor public school for boys. Ridiculous, really, Julian knows more about my father than he'll ever know about me.

'You'll be OK, Joyce, won't you, to drive on and off the ferry?'

'I'm not an advanced driver but, strange as it may seem, I've never experienced any difficulty driving up hill.'

Venning took a sideways glance at his wife's sJulian face. His own damn fault. He should have been more circumspect. There was no way Joyce was going to walk out on him, and Judith. The child would be heartbroken. Better do something about it. But what?

'Sorry to have to do it this way, darling, but I think it would be foolish not to move as quickly as possible.'

'Surely two more days wouldn't make any difference?'

'Hard to tell.'

'For Christ's sake, Julian, come clean. Why this unnecessary rush, all of a sudden?'

'Can't say, other than I have a gut feeling, and.......'

'And as we all know,' said Joyce bitterly, 'you're often right. This time, though, I think you've taken things too far. My father's nearly seventy, we know he's got this bee in his bonnet about vengeance, but when he actually gets there, if that's where he's gone, I'm sure it will fizzle out. He's no killer, Julian, I'm sure of that, but I would like to find him,' she added wistfully. 'And more than anything else in the world I'd like to see Mum, tell her I understand now. Understand why she tried to keep him at home. Poor Mum, why didn't she talk to me? Her illness, I'm sure, was psychosomatic. I could have helped her. Neither of my parents could communicate, and now, when it's too late I'm beginning to understand them, but why, why, why didn't Mum ever walk again after visiting Oradour?'

Venning said nothing. He knew.

There was surprisingly little traffic. Poitiers took them an hour and a half, and from thence they took the N10 towards Tours, which they by-passed, and continued on the N10 to Chartres.

'How about a short detour to Paradise, my darling? Have lunch at the Hostellerie St Jacques in Cloyes le Loir where the pilgrims stopped overnight on their way to Santiago de CompoEmily.'

'Sounds wonderful,' laughed Joyce, 'but I thought Santiago de CompoEmily was in Spain.'

'So it is. A long way to the shrine of St James, but distance means nothing to a determined pilgrim. You'll love the Hostellerie, the Patron, the food, the ambience, the wonderful watery expanse at the bottom of the garden. Another world hidden away, not on the Loire which everyone knows, but on the little Loir. Let's enjoy it, all part of our short honeymoon, but we'll return, my love.'

Joyce closed her eyes and smiled to herself. The pain had gone.

They were fortunate, arriving just in time to grab the last available table in the small dining room. Above the fireplace was a deer's head, with glassy eyes, and antlers nearly reaching the ceiling gazing down upon them. The diners were all French. A good sign, thought Venning, we'll be able to make a meal of it, as they do, and take two hours over lunch. Joyce must have been reading his thoughts.

'Knowing we have time on our hands, why don't we opt for the menu of the day?'

'If that suits you, my darling, then it suits me. It must be good otherwise the place wouldn't be full of locals.' He picked up the menu.

'Bouillabaisse, followed by coq au vin, or gibelotte, then the cheeseboard before finishing with mousse au chocolat, or pêches flambées.'

'What on earth, when it's at home, is gibelotte?'

'Rabbit stew.'

'Haven't come all this way to eat rabbit, so I'll settle for the soup, coq au vin, cheese, and mousse chocolat.'

'Wish this was our local,' sighed Venning, 'but then I guess we'd put on too much weight and die young.'

But Joyce didn't hear him. 'Julian what's the matter? Why the urgency, why the hurry? You've got to explain.'

He thought about it for some moments befoe answering. He didn't want to scare her.

'Mine's a funny business, darling. We often have to work on theories, feelings, presentiments. Without evidence there's no option. I know a little about your father, something of your childhood, your relationships at home, and Andrew's inability to talk about the past. If only he'd been able to communicate, let the aggro flow, not bottle it up, share his grief, we wouldn't be here now. He never talked. His colleagues at the office hardly knew him. Everything leads me to believe that if he finds this German he may go over the top and do something he'll regret.'

'But, Julian, be realistic, what are his chances?'

'Remote, I'd say. The percentage of airmen killed during the war was higher than in any other sphere, and if he wasn't killed he may already be dead from natural causes.'

'Oh God, I hope so. Dad has been thinking about this man for fifty years. What will happen if he can't find him?'

'There's no telling, but the sooner I locate Andrew, the sooner we can get back to our normal lives.'

'But this is your normal life. What's different!'

'Yes, yes I know, it isn't easy,' he said quietly.

The waiter who was about to clear away the soup plates saw the Englishman take his wife's hand and look at her as though seeing her for the first time. It was an inappropriate moment, thought the waiter, in a truly Gallic fashion, to interrupt.

'Darling, if I were free to tell you what I do, I would, but it's a mistake, in a job like mine to bring my work home with me. Home is a place where I can relax.'

'But you're not being truthful, Julian. You don't always leave it behind. You lie awake tossing and turning, and then you creep downstairs, have a whisky, and creep back again. Your breath gives you away. Now if you could talk about it, which is exactly what you're saying about Dad, then you too would be freer in your mind.'

What Venning couldn't and wouldn't ever divulge were the types of cases all policemen loathe. Child molestation, child murder, missing children. Joyce would be reminded again, and again of her own daughter, cruelly assaulted and murdered. He liked to shake off work when he closed the front door, but he must make an effort, talk to Joyce about some of the less harrowing cases. Their relationship was growing, but like everything in an English garden it needed constant attention, weeding, water, fertilisation, sunlight and temperate weather.

'Landing my problems on you isn't the answer. I think, perhaps, we should do more things together.'

'But you're never in.'

'I'll take more weekends off.'

'And the phone too,' she said quickly.

'No need. We'll go away. Down to West Dean in Sussex where we can learn how to do our own upholstery, restore antiques, paint, weave, make music, anything that takes your fancy.'

'I'll keep you up to that,' she said firmly. 'Upholstery, I think is the answer.'

'Do you know something, Julian,' said Joyce, as she swallowed her last mouthful of Brie, 'a pilgrim's journey must have been a medieval holiday.'

'Probably was,' laughed Venning, 'but if I'd been a pilgrim and been offered this sort of fare I would have given up, and stayed right here.'

'No, you wouldn't,' said Joyce quickly, 'not if you were you, because you can't give up. It's your nature, that's why you found Susan, and that is why you'll find Dad.'

She closed her eyes, but closing her eyes couldn't blot out the past, nor could she forget what she owed her husband. When she opened them again she looked at Venning seeing the same compassion in those deep blue eyes that had sustained her throughout the desperate hunt for Susan. She felt guilty.

'I'm sorry, Julian, sorry for being so tetchy.'

'A pity we have to leave,' said Venning. 'You could say we've been making a meal of it, but we'll be back, just as soon as we can.'

They made unbelievable progress, whistled through Dreux and Evreux, and picked up the motorway north of Louviers. The traffic into the ferry port was heavy, but they were in no hurry. They laughed at the antics of a traffic policeman who blew his whistle and waved his arms at the same time, causing chaos. They parked on the quay before wandering round the town, and taking a look at the Maison de la Culture, where they enjoyed a leisurely drink, before returning to the car. They watched the *Pride of Hampshire* ease into its accustomed berth, and disgorge its holiday makers, the French returning, the British about to begin.

'Julian, why don't you go now? It's 8.30 and there may not be too many trains to Paris.'

Venning gave her a quizzical look.

'Don't look at me like that. I'm quite capable, and I might even enjoy driving into the jaws of that monster.'

'All right, darling, I'll make tracks. Look after yourself, and drive carefully when you reach the other side. You're my most precious possession.'

Joyce threw her arms round his neck. 'I love you, my darling, and I'll take care.'

He knew Joyce would be safely back in England before he reached Berlin. There'd be time to ring her before his appointment. His step was light as he made his way to the taxi rank. St James had worked a miracle for the most unlikely of pilgrims. The Hostellerie St Jacques had been perfect.

'La gare, s'il vous plait. Je prends un train rapide pour Paris.'

'Bot! Les trains ne sont pas très rapides, Monsieur, vous savez....deux heures pour aller à Paris, ça, ce n'est pas tellement rapide!'

Venning laughed. 'Savez-vous, Monsieur, l'heure du prochain train?'

'Oui. Huit heures moins six! On est pressé!' he replied looking at his watch.

'Allors, allez-y!'

The taxi driver started the meter and the Inspector was driven at a blistering pace to the station. The Le Havre-Paris express was immaculately clean, extremely comfortable, took only two hours, and arrived on the dot at the Gare St Lazare. Venning couldn't make up his mind whether to take a room for the night or go direct to the airport and find a comfortable waiting room. The plane left at 0740, arriving at Tegel at 1030 hours--he might oversleep, and if he missed his appointment with a man like Dadswell he could be left kicking his heels for days. Discretion overcame the need for comfort.

The three hour flight to Berlin, with Air France, gave Venning time in which to re-think everything he'd learnt about Andrew Pringle, but how had he travelled? By plane, decided Venning, quite the easiest route into Berlin despite all the recent changes since re-unification. How well did the irascible Group Captain Dadswell know Andrew, and would ten minutes with the gentleman be enough? Would he know where Andrew was staying or anything of of his movements?

As the air hostesses cleared away the remains of breakfast the captain's voice came over the intercom.

'Mesdames, messieurs, ceci est votre Capitaine. Nous sommes à ce moment au dessus de la Forêt Noire, hauteur 10,000 mètres. Nous allons bientôt épouver des conditions turbulentes et je vous demande, pour votre sécurité et confort, de rester assis dans la cabine et d'attacher votre ceinture. Nous arriverons, à peu près, à l'heure attendue, malgré le temps qu'il fait.'

Venning closed his eyes and slept.

Francis Dadswell's morning began badly, as so many of his mornings did. During breakfast Angela mentioned, quite casually, that she'd invited half a dozen friends for cocktails and snacks, nothing too much, but enough in case any of them had decided to miss dinner.

'You'll be on you own, Angela. You know perfectly well I need more warning.'

'You've had plenty of warning.'

He looked at his wife in amazement, and then looked away quickly. It was a sight he couldn't abide so early in the day. There was something of the slut about Angela. Why on earth did she have to troll around in a dressing gown with her hair in those damned awful curlers looking like something out of *East Enders*? Much easier to go to the excellent hairdresser on the base. As for warning him about tonight's event, that was a nonsense, she'd said nothing.

'We have a system, Francis, which was your idea. There is a king sized calendar hanging on the notice board in the kitchen. All you have to do is look at it. Anyway, what are you doing tonight?'

'Going to the opera.'

'I should have known,' Angela sighed, 'you really are the pits.'

'Why does an educated woman need to use such damned awful expressions. All, I shouldn't wonder, picked up from that boring BBC soap you watch.'

Angela sniffed. 'As Rosemary takes so much trouble videoing English programmes for me, the least I can do is watch them.'

'Well it's a pity,' said her husband with his mouth full of toast, 'that you don't use your eyes a little more advantageously', and your tongue a little less, he thought to himself.

'What do you mean?'

'I always pin my theatre tickets on the board next to the diary. Have done for the past three years. All you have to do is **look**.'

'Well I didn't, so what are you going to do about my sin of omission?'

'Welcome your guests, of course, not with open arms, but with a bleak smile on my face, and then when they're well stuck into the latest dirt I'll make a quiet get-away, regretfully having missed the first act of *Lohengrin*.'

'No wonder your staff find you uncooperative.'

Dadswell dealt with the day's routine matters before his 10 o'clock appointment with two of Berlin's top policemen who were concerned about the escalation of the IRA's terrorist activities in West Germany. It was a workmanlike meeting with practical suggestions from both sides, but the discussion went on far longer than he'd anticipated. As he walked with them along the corridor leading from his office to the main staircase where his visitors took their leave, he saw Detective Inspector Venning sitting in the reception area on the floor below. Dammit, could have done without this fellow now, but ten minutes is what I said, with luck five should be enough. He returned to his office in a fractious mood, and gave instructions to his aide to have the visitor shown up at once, and after ten minutes, interrupt, say a car is waiting to take him to his luncheon appointment.

'Will you be wanting coffee, sir?'

'No we can do without that.'

The visitor was shown in, and the two men took stock of each other. The policeman in open neck shirt, blazer, and grey flannels looked totally at ease. He was used to this type of situation. A throw-back, thought Francis Dadswell. With his red hair and beard he could eaily be a Celtic warrior. Would even make an impressive Tristram if he could sing. Venning had not expected to find the RAF Officer dressed in civvies. Not even a regimental tie, but one of multi coloured silk in red, blue, and green which contrasted admirably with his pale grey shirt and expensive well cut dark grey suit, which sat easily on him. Quite a dresser this one, he thought.

'Sit down, Inspector, we have ten minutes before I leave for a luncheon appointment, so you'd better come to the point.'

It was no good, thought Venning, fobbing this man off with a thin story of a missing father-in-law. It was the truth or nothing.

'It's a long story, sir...'

'Not longer than ten minutes, I hope.'

'...and has its origins in March 1945, a few months before the war ended. I hesitate, Group Captain, to sound melodramatic, but I'm very much afraid that unless I find Andrew Pringle, my wife's father, as soon as possible he may ... he may do something disastrous. I'm afraid, sir, he may commit murder.'

Francis Dadswell almost sat to attention. 'Are you saying, Inspector, that Andrew Pringle is intent on assassination?'

'Yes.'

'I can't believe it. A cultured man, deeply appreciative of music. He seemed so balanced, equable, slightly reserved, and maybe it sounds a bit old fashioned, a gentleman, *a gentleman on whom I built an absolute trust.*'

'Macbeth Act 1.' said Venning softly.

They looked at each other and smiled. Suddenly the air was cleared. The two men felt comfortable with each other. Group Captain Dadswell pressed a switch and spoke to his aide. 'Coffee, at once Simmons.'

'Well, Mr Venning, you'd better tell me the story, then I can decide whether to help, which may be interference, or whether to remain neutral.'

'Andrew Pringle vanished from the face of the earth over a month ago leaving neighbours to look after the cat, and the car in the garage. Fortunately he left a couple of books with you which resulted in a note from Colin which my wife and I read week. We were both amazed to learn that Andrew had taken a crash course in German and would be calling on you.'

'Well, he could hardly continue with his research unless he'd mastered the language.'

'Research?'

'Yes, for the book he's writing.'

'Book,' murmured Venning. 'He's not writing a book, sir, but I'll guarantee he's researching in depth.'

'What does that mean?'

'Let me try and explain what has been happening. Joyce was in such a state over her father's disappearance that I decided the only way forward was to read everything in the house we could lay our hands on. It was, after all, our only clue to the present. I won't go into all the background that we managed to unravel except to give you a résumé of Andrew's early life. He and his twin brother Peter, served in the RAF during the war. Flew in the same squadron, but latterly in different planes. Andrew was a pilot and Peter a navigator. In March 1945 the Germans launched *Operation Giselle* using Junkers 88 fighters. Their orders were to infiltrate squadrons of British bombers returning to England after raids on German towns, and stay with them until they reached their home base. They were then ordered to attack the planes when they were at their most vulnerable, the moment, in fact, of landing. Andrew was in the air preparatory to landing when he saw Peter's plane attacked. It exploded in mid air. From that moment he vowed vengeance upon the German pilot who had murdered his brother, but his wife by various stratagems kept him at home always refusing to holiday abroad. She became a permanent invalid and for a time the idea of vengeance faded, at least that's what Joyce and I have gleaned from his letters and diaries. Then at long last when he seemed on an even keel Emily, his wife, agreed to spend three weeks in France. She was in a wheelchair, but had for the first time for years been managing a few steps. On their fourth night they stayed at the Lion D'or, in Limoges. They asked the patron of the hotel to suggest places of interest, not too far, that they could visit. Oradour was top of the list.'

'Oh my God,' whispered the Captain.

'The visit totally destroyed them both. Emily never walked again, and on the back of a photograph Andrew had taken in the cemetery he'd written, *The sun should never shine* which I couldn't understand until I too visited Oradour.'

'Excuse me, sir,' said Simmons as he made a noisy entrance. 'Your car is waiting.'

'You can cancel my luncheon appointment, Simmons. Apologise and say we'll try again next week.'

'Very good, sir.'

'What, Inspector, has the sun to do with all this?'

'The massacre took place on a brilliantly sunny day in June, 1945. Andrew's visit also took place on a hot sunny day, and only two days ago when my wife and I were there, the same conditions prevailed. A cloudless brilliant blue sky-- a sunny afternoon in June,-- God's in his heaven all's right with the world--an agricultural village at peace--children in school--

invalids in their beds, when an avalanche of evil descended upon the unsuspecting villagers. That's what Andrew couldn't stomach, and for evermore on a brilliantly sunny day he would remember Oradour, but more than that, it recreated an overwhelming desire for vengeance.'

'It was a mistake,' said Dadswell, 'or so I've been led to believe.'

'What was?'

'There's a story that the boche should have destroyed Oradour-sur-Vayres, a village only 25 kilometeres distance from Oradour-sur-Glane. The Germans were stunned by the unexpected 'D' Day landings in Normandy. Hitler desperately needed troop reinforcements, and ordered the Second Panzer Division, based in the south of France, to Normandy. He expected it to arrive at the Channel within two days, but he'd reckoned without the French Resistance, who thwarted the Germans at every turn. Railway and road bridges blown up, roads mined, troops harrassed. The two days became three weeks during which time horrific punishing reprisals were suffered by the civilian population. It was a hard time, Mr Venning, hard for the French, the Americans, the British, and hard too for the average German conscript who must have wondered why he'd become fodder to satisfy a madman's dreams. My father, was fodder too, a major in the Royal Artillery, whom I don't remember, killed during the British landings at Ouistreham. Killed on June 7th, 'D' Day plus one.'

Venning looked at the man in front of him and wondered what it was like to have been brought up hearing constant stories of one's historical father?

'Now, Mr Venning,' said Francis Dadswell, 'we'd better have lunch, not in the mess, I think, but in this office where we can talk unreservedly about Andrew Pringle and decide on a modus operandi which must take priority over everything else in hand. We must stop him before he creates an international incident.'

'I hope it won't come to that. Let's hope his quarry has died naturally.'

'Simmons,' barked the Captain over the intercom, 'get Chambers to set a table for two in here. A working lunch, you understand, and no interruptions.'

In the next office Lieutenant Simmons stared at the small speaker on his desk in astonishment. What dreadful event had occurred to cause his boss to cancel lunch at the Ambassador Hotel? A weekly happening where he met up with several of his buddies, rarely returning to the office in the afternoon. Once the table was set, complete with a bottle of Hock on ice, a hostess trolley was wheeled in and left alongside the table.

'Will there be anything else, sir?'

'No, Chambers. This will do admirably.'

'Talk about your father-in-law, Mr Venning. What sort of man is he?'

'I hardly know him. Joyce and I have been married for less than a year, and during that time we've met on no more than half a dozen occasions. My wife would also tell you that she scarcely knows her father, something she regrets. We have been desperately worried about him, so worried, in fact, that we've been driven to reading his private papers in the hope that they'd give us a lead. By perusing his letters we have, to some extent, been successful in recreating his past. The past, as I have said before, is the only clue we have to the present. My wife was exceedingly shaken, when she discovered her father, whom she'd always believed to be an only child, had a twin brother. He's a very secret man.'

'It may seem strange to you, Mr Venning, but during Andrew's stay in Berlin, nearly a fortnight, you know, we found genuine rapport and respect. Our interests are similar, both being opera buffs. Andrew's into Verdi and the Italian scene, a bit too too florid I'm afraid, and I'm into Wagner and Richard Strauss. However, I introduced Andrew to *The Mastersingers* and he made arrangements to take me to a performance of *Un Ballo in Maschera*, an opera I've never seen. I didn't go. Later I regretted disappointing him, but it was a sudden decision. I made the usual excuses....army business and so forth, but he didn't believe me.'

Francis Dadswell sipped his wine thoughtfully. 'Strangely enough, Mr Venning, I thoroughly enjoyed your father-in-law's company, and could never describe him as uncommunicative. We were good for each other. We widened our horizons. We also played tennis and for a man of nearly seventy he has a devastating serve. However, I got my own back when he joined me on the rifle range. At snap shooting he didn't make a single hit, but in aiming at a stationary target... '

'Good God, sir, you don't mean he has a gun!'

'No. No, he didn't have a gun. In fact he hadn't used one since the war. He was no slouch, though, and after an hour's practice with a Smith and Wesson he got his eye in, enjoying himself in the process.'

'What happened to the revolver?'

'Sergeant Fletcher returned it to the armoury.'

Venning found himself wondering whether Andrew had managed to get his hands on a gun.

'There is only one thing I found slightly disturbing....' he hesitated.

'Go on, sir.'

'I really wasn't expecting, as I have said, to have such......such rapport with your father-in-law. When Colin, whom you've met, of course, rang me and asked me to help Andrew with his research he was quite off putting. Told me Andrew was a taciturn, reserved man, an ex-colleague of his who was writing a book about the RAF and needed back-up material covering the 39-45 War. It was easy. Within hours of Andrew's arrival in Berlin I'd made all the necessary contacts for him at the Staatsbibliothek, and welcomed him into my home. Now all this time I was under the impression, must have been something Colin said, that he'd been commissioned to write a book on the RAF. It came as quite a shock to learn that he thought it unlikely his book would ever see the light of day because he hadn't even approached a publisher. A little disconcerting, to be sure, because by this time, of course, I'd produced more contacts for him, and I too was embroiled in the myth of a commissioned book. One thing I abhor, Mr Venning, is being inaccurate.'

The Inspector nodded sympathetically. Francis Dadswell had stopped short of actually using the word 'lying.'

'Have you any idea where Andrew is at this moment?'

'He may be at Freiburg, that's where he said he was going.'

'What's at Freiburg?'

'The Militärgeschichtliches Forschungsamt, in other words military archives. Freiburg is a very beautiful spot. It's the tourist centre for the Shwarzwald, the Black Forest. And there's another thing......'

'Yes?'

'I don't like leading our German allies up the garden path.'

'Go on, sir.'

'Well, over the years I've become acquainted with Brigadier Doctor Erlbach, who is Chief of the Record Office. He's an erudite and kindly man who agreed to produce a Reader's Ticket for Andrew and give him all the assistance he required.'

'Could we check with the Doctor Erlbach, see if he's still working there?'

'Indeed we could.'

'When, did Andrew leave Berlin?'

'Nearly two weeks ago, I'd say.'

'How long will it take me to get there?'

'Too long.' The Captain pressed a button.

'Simmons!'

'Yes, sir?'

'Let me know the time of the next flight from Tegel to Basle, and get Brigadier Erlbach on the line.'

'Very good, sir.'

Venning laughed. 'One of my greatest pleasures in life is to see a man doing his job to perfection. Doesn't matter whether he's a potter, a carpenter, a pianist, an electrician or a Colonel.'

'What a pity, Mr Venning, that we're like ships that pass---no, perhaps we're not--if you don't find Andrew you must contact me immediately. I don't want a contretemps with the Germans. Incidentally how's your German?'

'A first, at Lampeter.'

'Excellent. I'd like to be a fly on the wall watching a policeman at work!'

'Touché.'

The phone rang. 'It'll be Doctor Erlbach.' Francis Dadswell lifted the phone and motioned Venning to pick up the extension. 'Guten Tag to you Brigadier. Tell me my friend, and forgive my brusqueness, is Andrew Pringle still using your excellent facilities?'

'No, Captain. He was here for only two days.'

'Have you any idea where he went?'

'None at all. He asked the librarian on duty to pass on his thanks to me, but he was in a hurry to leave, and I was in the middle of a meeting.'

'A pity because his daughter needs to contact him. The matter, I gather, is urgent. Would you be free tomorrow, Doctor Erlbach, to see a colleague of mine who will be in your neck of the woods, and needs to contact Andrew Pringle?'

'I have a meeting at 0930 hours, but we should be through by 1100 hours. Tell your colleague he's welcome. What's his name?'

The Inspector hastily put his hand over the extension mouthpiece and whispered 'Julian.'

'Venning, Julian Venning.'

'Good. Tell Herr Venning I'll be expecting him.'

The plane touched down at Basle at 1730, and the hire car which Venning had ordered before leaving Tegel was ready for him. Safer to have wheels. He'd plenty of time on his hands, no need to hare up the A5 motorway. The slower A98 direct from Switzerland to Freiburg would bring memories flooding back, but what the hell!

The traffic was heavy leaving the city, all those rich gnomes returning to their pads in the mountains. As he passed a sign indicating Lörrach to the right he remembered visiting a spectacular castle there when he and Rhoda were on their honeymoon. They married only two days after their degree finals, and then spent six weeks touring Switzerland and Germany in an old bone shaker his father had lent him. Further north on the A98 he saw the sign to Kandern famous for its bakeries and extravagant specialities, and it was in Kandern they'd spent a week at the Gasthaus while awaiting their results. They were in the middle of dinner when his father had phoned. A second for Rhoda in history and English literature, and a first in modern languages for Julian Venning. What a night that was! They felt like climbing mountains which is exactly what they did!

A few days later they found themselves on the main road to Freiburg with the towering *Belchen*) nearly 5000 feet to the west of them. Rhoda insisted on visiting the nearby Roman baths at Badenweiler, built by the Emperor Vespasian in the 1st century AD, and considered the finest example north of the Alps. Venning felt tempted to make the detour, but put the thought behind him, and put his foot down instead. He needed to get to Freiburg while it was still light, find a hotel, and get a meal. He was starving.

He was in luck. Owing to a cancellation the *Rappen* in Münsterplatz had a single room, and dinner was still being served. The waitress, a buxom fair haired country lass, was a great talker. Between courses she gave Venning the low down on all the British guests who'd stayed in the hotel over the past fortnight. No, she'd definitely not seen a tall thin elderly man with a shock of grey hair who wore glasses, only for reading.

Suddenly the Inspector felt tired and realised how he'd stretched the day from an early start in Paris to his overnight stop on the edge of the Black Forest. Bed was the only answer.

Brigadier Erlbach looked at his visitor in surprise. 'Perhaps I'm being obtuse, Herr Venning, but I can't quite fathom why information about Herr Pringle's research should help you to find him.'

'It probably won't, but there's a faint chance that it might give me a lead to his next port of call.'

'There is nowhere else in Germany where he could possibly find the information he needs. If it's of any help, he was writing a history of the RAF during the 39-45 War, and quite rightly, like all historians was cross checking his references against our records, to add verisimilitude.'

'I have the feeling,' said Venning carefully, 'that the last year of the war was causing him the most problems. The German raids, for instance, on RAF bases, sort of hit and run tactics. Luftwaffe fighters insinuating themselves into returning packs of bombers,'

Erlbach smiled at the layman's phraseology, which is exactly what Venning had intended.

'Ah! You are talking about *Operation Giselle*.'

'Could be,' said Venning non committally.

'Let us have a word with Colonel Fassbinder, our Director of Information and Education. He or a member of his staff may have helped Herr Pringle to locate the necessary files.'

Doctor Erlbach led the way to the library where three weeks earlier Andrew Pringle had completed his research. The Brigadier introduced the two men.

'You will excuse me, Herr Venning, if I leave you in Doctor Fassbinder's care. He knows everything that goes on here. Never misses a thing, but if there's any other way we can help, please don't hesitate to ask.'

Doctor Erlbach hurried back to take another look at the graphics being prepared for his monograph on the use of the tank.

'What exactly do you want to know, sir?' asked the German.

'It's not so much what I want to know, it's more a question of what did my father-in-law want to know.'

Doctor Fassbinder frowned, hadn't quite taken it in.

'Sorry, ' said Venning instantly, 'I haven't put that very well. An urgent family matter has cropped up and I need to discover the whereabouts of my father-in-law immediately.'

The German looked even more perplexed. 'But why should I be able to help you?'

'Because, if you can remember what he was researching I might be able to glean a few clues. You see his research won't have stopped here. He will go on and on until he finds what he's seeking.'

'There's no problem in looking at his area of research because it's all on record. The archive is held in the Bundesarchiv which means readers have to file their requests with my assistant who feeds the information into this computer.'

Wonderful, thought Venning. I didn't realise it would be so easy.

'I do know,' said the Doctor, 'what Herr Pringle's interests were, because we discussed the matter at some length on the day he arrived. He required information about Fighter Command's operations during the last four and a half months of the war. January to half way through May to be exact, with a special interest in *Operation Giselle*. Four and a half months entailed a lot of reading, a mountain of reading, Herr Venning, but he only spent five days here.'

I'm not surprised, thought the Inspector. All my damned father-in-law wanted was information about *Giselle*, the rest was cover.

'Is it possible Colonel Fassbinder for me to have a quick browse through the papers he was reading?'

'That is no problem, Herr Venning. German archives are available to any serious minded scholar who wants to study them, and it seem to me that your search, if not for the Holy Grail, is a serious business. Make yourself comfortable while I pick Ludwig's brains.'

'Ludvig?'

'My computer!'

Doctor Fassbinder tapped away as fast as any typist. 'Ah, here we are. The files for January 1945 until the end of the war were requested on the Thursday and delivered here by 0900 hours on the Friday.'

He took a closer look at the screen. 'That's odd,' he muttered to himself,

'Very odd!'

'What's the matter, sir?'

'Mr Pringle returned all the files on the following Monday with the exception of Fighter Command's Operations for March and April. We don't work Saturdays and Sundays which means he couldn't possible have read everything in a day.'

It was not surprising, thought Venning, that the good Doctor was frowning.

'Ah, more entries,' he said, as he gazed at screen. 'He requested Nijmegen Station's Debriefing Combat Report for April 2nd and 3rd, 1945. Herr Pringle must have been making a very detailed study.'

'It's an area,' said Venning slowly, 'in which he has shown great interest, and information, I gather, is sparse in England. He will have valued your help and expertise.'

'What I can't fathom, Herr Venning.....' Doctor Fassbinder stopped in mid flow, and stared at the computer in amazement...'

'Why don't you share your thoughts, Doctor?'

'First of all, I can't see how you expect to find Herr Pringle by sifting through his research material. And now I find he also put in a written request for the Photographic Records. I'd better have a word with Leutnant Lösemann.' Doctor Fassbinder picked up the phone. 'That you Lösemann? Good. I need you in here at once.'

The fair haired, clean shaven young officer entered at the double. 'Yes, Colonel?'

'I see you've recorded Herr Pringle's interest in Nijmegen's Debriefing Combat Files?

'Yes, sir.'

'So why weren't they abstracted?'

'He was only interested in the de-briefing on the night of......'

'April 2nd and 3rd,' said Venning.

'Yes, sir.'

'So what did you do about it Leutnant? asked Doctor Fassbinder.

'I ran it off on the computer for him. He was in a hurry and planned to leave the next morning.'

'I see,' but the baffled Doctor Fassbinder clearly didn't see. 'And what about the Photographic Records?'

'They won't be available until Wednesday, so he said not to bother.'

'Thank you Leutnant, that will be all.'

The Leutnant hesitated. 'Sir.........'

'Yes, Lösemann?'

'He read through the Combat Report, and then asked for the Personnel File for the Nijmegen Station.'

'You didn't run that off as well, did you Leutnant?'

'He asked for an extract, sir. It only took five minutes.'

'Did he say why he wanted it?'

'He'd hoped for a personal interview with Oberleutnant Josef Marx who'd be on a mission on the night of April 2nd, but he was out of luck, sir. Oberleutnant Marx died two years ago.'

'Thankyou Leutnant. That is all I need to know.' Venning gave a sigh of relief. There wasn't much damage Andrew could do now .

Doctor Fassbinder shook his head. 'It's always difficult to track down ex-pilots, and as you can see they are becoming fewer and fewer. 'I don't think we can help you, Herr Venning. Your father-in-law could be anywhere in the country.'

Venning had an unexpected flash of inspiration. Never underestimate Andrew.

'There could have been other pilots, sir, worth interviewing. How long would it take to run off copies of the extracts my father-in-law requested?'

'It's that urgent, is it Herr Venning.'

'A matter of life and death, sir.

'It should only take a few minutes. Doctor Fassbinder hummed as he typed the instructions. He sat back and waited with a half smile on his face.

Venning looked at his watch as the German handed him the copies.

'Three and half minutes, sir. Congratulations.'

SEVEN

Detective Inspector Julian Venning fairly flew down the stairs of the Militärgeschichtliches Forschungsamt and into a restaurant on the ground floor where he settled himself at a corner table and ordered a jug of black coffee before scanning the print-out Doctor Fassbinder had given him. Intuition had always been the Inspector's strongest weapon. He knew he was right about Andrew. His father-in-law wasn't interested in Oberleutnant Marx, alive or dead. His interest lay in the whereabouts of Oberleutnant Helmut Schmidt, the pilot who'd successfully used cloud cover to sneak, unnoticed, into a pack of returning aircraft. Guts, thought Venning, what guts that must have taken. Deserved the V.C. for an operation like that. Wonder what the German equivalent is, and what he actually got for destroying three enemy aircraft and bringing his own plane safely home?

He poured himself another cup of coffee before looking at the Personnel extract. The Schmidts like the Smiths were there in abundance, but only two merited attention. The first one had been wounded in action over the Mediterranean and was doing a desk job at Nijmegen, but the second was the man he wanted. No! The man Andrew wanted. No address. Fortunate in a way, slowed things up a bit, but he didn't underestimate his father-in-law. Helmut Schmidt, it seemed, had in his off duty periods been studying Local Government Law, in the hope that he'd be able to find a job at the Rathaus in Wittlich. Unlikely, mused Venning, that he'd been able to choose where he wanted to work, and even if he'd been one of the lucky ones, would he, after nearly half a century, be living in the same area? It was a slender thread, but his only option.

Back in the hotel he sat on his bed and made several phone calls. There were no resources on which to call. No back-up. No way he could go to the police. A politically unsound move because the Media would get hold of it and have a field day. There was no time to muck about. Francis Dadswell must provide some of the answers.

'You've caught me just in time, Mr Venning. What's the problem?'

'I need the address of an ex-Luftwaffe pilot who was with Fighter Command and stationed near Nijmegen in 1945.'

'Ex-pilot,' murmured the Group Captain. 'Quickest way, I guess, is to connect with the Aircrew Association. Leave it with me. I'll get Simmons on to it straight away.'

'There's a faint possibility that he might be living in the Wittlich area.'

'Really! A splendid place to live. I know it well. We've spent many long week ends there on the banks of the Moselle tasting the splendours of the incomparable white grape which grows in abundance on the gentle hills.'

Venning could have done without the eulogy, but he'd have to play along.

'You wax lyrical, sir.'

'Pity you haven't time to do the tour.'

'The tour?'

'Of the vineyards and wine cellars. There's nothing better, Inspector, than a Bernkastel Eiswein, nectar of the Gods, but I'm digressing, let's get back to the matter in hand.'

Thank God for that, thought Venning.

'Wittlich is about 170 miles from Freiburg. There are some excellent hotels....'

'No such luxury,' interrupted Venning. 'From now on I'll be staying in Gasthauses. This operation is proving expensive.'

'Yes, yes, I'm sure. Give me your number, and I'll get Simmons to ring you back within the hour.'

'Thanks.' At least he didn't hang about.

He dialled Oxford direct. Judith answered the phone.

'You all right, Jude?'

'Daddy,!' she shrieked. 'Daddy, we broke up yesterday and Mummy took me to the fair, and I won a goldfish.'

'What for?'

'Rolling a 10p on to the right number.'

'How many tenpences did you have to spend?'

'Only six.'

Venning laughed. 'And how did you get him home?'

'In a plastic bag, but he's in a pudding basin until I get proper goldfish bowl for him.

'Is Mummy there?'

'Yes,' answered Joyce. 'I'm upstairs on the extension.'

She sounded different, more cheerful.

'We had a card yesterday from Dad, but I couldn't ring you, didn't know your number.' Venning didn't miss the implied criticism. He's OK, Julian, he's OK. Told us not to worry.'

He's OK, thought Venning gloomily, but what about Helmut Schmidt?

'Where's it from? What's the postmark?'

'Trier.'

'And Daddy, ' interrupted Judith, 'it's got a picture of a Roman arena on the front, where they used to fight lions.'

'When was it posted?'

'Three days ago. Have you had any luck, Julian?'

'The usual amount of luck, and the usual amount of plod,' he said wearily, 'but by tomorrow I should be a lot further forward. It's no good giving you this number because I'm leaving today, but I'll call tomorrow. Look after yourselves. Bye, my darlings,' he said rather abruptly and replaced the receiver.

He dashed down to the car waving at the young woman in reception as he went through the entrance hall, and a few seconds later she watched as he rushed up the stairs again.

These English, she thought, there's never enough time for them. He spread the map on the bed. Yes, Trier was exactly where he expected it to be, not too far from Luxembourg, but, and he couldn't believe his good fortune, only 30 kilometres from Wittlich.

The phone rang.

'Yes?'

'Reception here, sir. There's a call for you.'

'Mr Venning?' Simmons sounded rather distant. 'I've got what you wanted. Have you a pencil to hand.'

'Yes, fire away, Lieutenant.'

'The address you need is Brauhaus, Burgstrasse, Bernkastel. Fortunately he's not ex-directory. The code is 06531 and the number 88821.'

'Thank you, Lieutenant. That's excellent news.'

'A pleasure, sir. And, sir, Group said to ring him if there's anything else he can do.

Interesting, thought Venning as he replaced the phone. Was Andrew in Bernkastel or Trier, only half an hour away by road?

Trier might have taken half an hour by car, but not travelling by local bus as Andrew Pringle had done only five days before. He'd not been in a hurry. His appointment was midday at the Roman Amphitheatre in Trier with instructions to look like a tourist. Gunther, whose surname had never been divulged, was his contact. Buying a gun was harder than he'd imagined. German regulations were rigid. Two licences had to be acquired, from the local town hall, the Kriesverwaltung. One for the firearm, and one for ammunition. On top of that the applicant needed to have a damn good reason for carrying a gun; living in an isolated farm house; transporting vast amounts of money; driving a high powered executive who could either be held to ransom or killed by terrorists. Going through the official channels had never entered his mind, but it had taken nearly a week, going quietly about his task, to ferret out the whereabouts of a dealer in small arms. A dealer who was prepared to sell his merchandise at highly inflated prices to a stranger. Andrew wasn't interested in Gunther. Didn't want to know his name, nor where he lived, but he was interested in making sure the merchandise worked, and there was only one way.....try it out. Would the German be agreeable? If not, the deal was off, and he'd have to start from square one all over again.

Gunther Hagen, a small insignificant man loved his hardware which he kept cleaned, oiled, and polished. He also hated having to part with his favourite pieces. But he had to live. Four young mouths to feed and a voracious wife. Gunther wasn't a tough man. He'd had to work hard to produce the right image. There was no room for mistakes in his job. He had to weigh up his client, assess the risk, and then he'd talk to the would-be assassin in MacDonalds over a mug of coffee, make sure there was no foul up before he dared display his wares. The Englishman, he'd been told, didn't know too much, didn't seem to know exactly what he wanted. An old man, his contact had said.

Andrew would have liked more time in Trier. A few days in which to enjoy the oldest city in Germany, time to climb high above the city to view the Porta Nigra, a massive structure once the northern gate to the Roman Empire. Augustus, it is said, founded the city in 15BC, but the Celts were there first, and before them the Assyrians. He must forget ancient civilisations and concentrate on the business in hand. He'd no idea what Gunther looked like, but Gunther would know him. A waiter in that sleazy bar had taken a poloroid as he sat drinking a stein of lager.

He looked at his watch. Five minutes past the hour. Where was the man? All these people milling around were tourists, their cameras at the ready, and guide books in their hands. He stiffened as a voice behind him asked whether he was Herr Pringle.

'Yes, yes I am Herr Pringle,' he said as he turned round to find himself looking down on the head of a small compact man whose hands were empty.

'No, no I never carry anything,' said the German reading his thoughts.

The grey eyes were watchful. Gunther turned full circle as if examining the ancient walls, but his eyes missed nothing. No, there were no police around.

'Herr Pringle,' he said softly, 'let us walk into the town, five minutes, that's all, and we'll discuss your problem in MacDonalds.'

Without a word Andrew followed him. The German stopped suddenly and pointed to a vomitorium. 'Someone is taking an interest in us. Look as if you're interested, Herr Pringle.'

'But I am,' protested Andrew.

'They knew how to build, did those Romans. Look at that brickwork, we can't better that even today,' said Gunther grinning.

A grinning diminutive arms dealer with an unfortunate giggle was not what Andrew had been expecting. Perhaps he'd read too many Deightons and Forsythes?

When they reached MacDonalds Gunther sat down waiting for his client to purchase the coffees. Oh yes, thought Andrew, he's been through this ritual many times before. The German used his own simple method of assessing this strange Englishman who had flitted into his life for a brief moment, and who would be gone just as quickly to follow whatever foul purpose he had in mind.

Gunther sipped his coffee and said nothing for five minutes. Odd, extremely odd, this elderly grey haired man wasn't in the least rattled. He sat there patiently, no angst, no sweat, no looking around to see if he was being watched. Gunther was intrigued. What had this man in his mind, and what was he going to do? The imperturbability and the repose was frightening.

'Well, Herr Pringle,' said the German provider looking him straight in the eyes,' what sort of weapon do you require?'

The Englishman half smiled. 'You know, I'm not quite sure. I was hoping you could tell me.'

Gunther frowned. 'What distance? A stationary or moving target? And how big is the target?'

'I imagine,' said Andrew slowly, 'that the target will be no taller than I am, probably stationary, and hopefully face to face.'

God, this man's cool, thought Gunther.

'I'd also need a little practice if possible. Be safer.'

'Safer for who?' sniggered Gunther.

'Well, I don't want to make a mess of it, do I? The job has to be done.'

'I think, Herr Pringle, you could do with a small revolver, probably a Smith and Wesson, or a Walther, and I think you should use a silencer. Precautions cost a little more, but pay dividends.'

'Yes, yes, I suppose that it is a good idea, normally, but this is a one-off, you understand. I shall dump the gun when I've finished with it.'

'A waste of a good piece, Herr Pringle. Maybe, I could buy it back, a quarter of its price, you understand?'

'No. There won't be time for that. Now, are we going to get down to business?'

'I am taking you for a ride, Herr Pringle. My car's in the square. We'll be going up into the hills beyond Waldrach. A farm there, well hiddden, where a little revolver practice worries only the cows.

Andrew breathed deeply. This was it...so nearly there.

There was nothing wrong with the engine of Gunther's battered old Volkswagen which he wasn't using to advantage.

'I always drive carefully, Herr Pringle, best not to attract attention, but there's enough under the bonnet if it's ever needed.'

Andrew wasn't worried how the man drove as long as they reached the farm safely. He'd turned off, wasn't listening any more. The hills reminded him of Wales and with total recall he thought about Peter, about the holidays they'd enjoyed as children. He remembered how his mother always packed a large trunk which was collected a few days before their holiday began, and how, quite miraculously, it was waiting for them when they arrived at their grandfather's cottage. It was a long train journey from Northampton to Aberdovey, adventurous too, because they had to change at Crewe. On one occasion, he remembered it as clearly as if it had been yesterday, his mother hustled them off the LMS train at Crewe, and they changed platforms to wait for a GWR going west. She'd collected all their gear together before they alighted, their crayons, drawing pads, a game of Halma, sandwiches they hadn't eaten, and a thermos which she thrust into his father's hands while she gathered up their raincoats and souwesters because it always rained in Aberdovey in August. As the train pulled away she gave a shriek. "Oh my God! The chocolate roll! It's still on the train." Tears poured down her face. Pete had reacted at once. He reached up and put his arms round her neck.

"Don't worry, Mum. We can buy Gran another one."

"No, we can't. That chocolate roll was fresh and filled with real cream. Fresh from Adams' Corner Shop. It's Gran's special treat. She always looks forward to it. Nobody makes chocolate roll like that."

His father came to the rescue. "Come on old lady, it's not the end of the world. We'll buy her the largest bunch of flowers we can find."

And that holiday, the wettest he could remember, when large black slugs had the mountains to themselves, Gran had to be content with flowers.

Gunther suddenly pulled off the road, and into a lay-by keeping his eyes on the road.

'What's the matter?

'Nothing, I hope, Herr Pringle, but there's a red Porsche, a couple of cars behind, which has been with us since we left Trier, and no one in their right mind buys a Porsche to trundle along at the speed we're doing. You stay in the car while I take a look.'

Andrew didn't have any option. Gunther was out of the car and lost to view amid the vines. The German approached the farm cautiously. So far, so good. No cars parked in front of the farmhouse. No unusual activity. Now for a look at the yard. He circled the house until he could see the old stables on the east of the farmyard. Only the familiar farm vehicles and a motor cycle which he knew belonged to Farmer Speer's eldest boy.

The man sitting in the passenger seat heard the voices of two men approaching the car some seconds before he actually saw them. *Christ! I'm an idiot. All this money on me. It's a put up job.* Quickly he locked all the doors, closed the windows, and slid his wallet under the passenger seat. The two men, both with rucksacks on their backs, took a good look at the car, and nodded to him as they passed. He breathed a sigh of relief. It's my damn nerves, he thought, working overtime.

Gunther also watched their progress along the road and waited until they were out of sight before returning to the car. He noted with approval the closed windows, and assumed the doors were locked. Careful this Englishman. Didn't behave like an amateur, but he had to be otherwise he wouldn't be buying his shooter in Trier. He would have nipped over the border into Belgium where no licence was needed, no questions asked, and where an up-to-date lightweight model would have cost him no more than 400 marks.

Seeing the two men made Andrew realise just how vulnerable he was. No one in the world knew he was here. The farmhouse was remote. His wallet held 2000 marks and all his credit cards, and he was unarmed. A sitting duck. Gunther eased the car down a narrow track hidden by tall hedges on both sides, and driving round the farmhouse made for the open stable. Once they were inside Farmer Speer closed the massive doors behind them. This is it, thought Andrew.

'They're on the ball here,' said Gunther with a laugh. 'Now then, Herr Pringle, we'll slink through this door into the barn. Farmer Speer, doesn't allow his wife to see who comes and goes, nor will he have her mixed up in this...this trading. His sons are another matter. I think they need the excitement, farming's a very dull occupation. We will stay in the barn until you've made your choice, and then when Speer gives us the all-clear we'll slip quietly away.' He ushered Andrew through the small door closing it behind them, before switching on the feeblest of lights.

'That's not much good, is it? muttered Andrew.

'You haven't seen anything yet.'

'Not likely to in this light.'

As Andrew's eyes became acclimatised he realised the barn was chock-a-block with bales of straw. Hardly a space in which to stand, let alone take aim. It's all a con, he thought grimly. I'll never get out of this place alive. His father's advice was coming home to roost. *Don't go beyond the bounds old son, you could be hoist.*

'Step back a bit, Herr Pringle,' came the order, 'and stand close to me.'

Andrew moved slowly keeping his eye on the door they'd just entered. The German pressed a button on the small gadget he was holding which produced a loud whirring noise as the floor beneath them shook and moved downwards.

'Keep still, Herr Pringle,' said Gunther sharply. 'The lift is only a metre square. You could get hurt.'

The lift, more like a stage trap, stopped.

Gunther tugged at Andrew's arm. 'Quickly, my friend, we don't want to leave a gaping hole.'

As they stepped off he pressed a button and the straw covered floor returned to its seemingly innocuous position in the badly lit barn.

The lighting under the barn was anything but feeble. Neon tubes illuminated every corner leaving nothing to the imagination. No one could mistake the function of this large basement room. Targets at forty feet, thirty feet, twenty feet, all adjustable. An area for snap shooting, and shop window dummies, dressed and undressed who were the unwitting victims, silently and patiently awaiting execution.

Gunther giggled. 'Everyone is surprised. Choose your man. Ferdinand, the male model with the red hair, dressed in evening clothes, turns most people on. They all like taking a pot shot at him. Or how about that nude over there with the big boobs?

The Englishman ignored the salacious remarks as he strolled over to a tall heavily built figure with blue eyes, dressed in a tweed jacket, and straw hat.'

'That's Hermann, tittered Gunther, 'keep meaning to find him some trousers. He finds it cold in the Winter.'

'He'll do,' said Andrew who was getting heartily sick of the inane giggle. 'Now let me take a look at what's on offer.'

He watched as Gunther unlocked a large steel cupboard, and opened a drawer containing a dozen revolvers.

'I thought you said they were hard to come by.'

'I did, but that was only sales talk. I can show you Berettas, Lugers, Walthers, Smith and Wessons, but how about this one?' Gunther giggled again, before carefully and lovingly selecting a pistol polished in a non-reflective matt blue with a chequered walnut grip.

'This little beauty is my favourite,' he said, as he stroked its surface. 'It's heavy, mind you, weighs over 1000 grams and is perfect for right handed assassins.' Gunther took a sideways look at Andrew, carefully noting his reaction to the word assassin. Yes, exactly what he'd thought. This man was shocked. Hadn't thought of himself as a killer. Andrew pulled himself together. He held out his hand for the gun.

'What is it?'

'An Italian job, A Bernadelli. Carries a 16 round box magazine in the butt.'

'Good God! I don't need 16 rounds. He put it down and picked up a slightly smaller pistol.

'That's a lovely piece,' cooed Gunther. 'A Walther P88. Carries 15 rounds in the butt, has a short recoil and suits an ambidextrous man.'

'I've told you I want something smaller, and I am totally right handed.'

'How about this?' He held a small revolver at arms length. 'It's a Llama Piccolo, small, concealable, and meant for personal defence. It's a man-stopper, all right.'

Andrew shook his head violently. At that moment he hated Gunther, hated the cool nonchalant manner in which he disposed of his lethal armoury. Stroking them, cooing over them, looking at them with as much love as a small boy lavishes on his first train set.

'What's that small gun in the corner of the drawer?' he rasped.

'That's a Colt, Mr Pringle, a Mustang 380 automatic which is a favourite with police officers. Can be easily concealed and only carries 5 rounds. As far as ladies in the States are concerned it's a useful toy they carry in their handbags. There's only one problem the short butt makes a full hand-grip impossible, but you may feel the advantage of being able to hide it in the palm of your hand outweighs all other considerations.'

Could slip it in his jacket pocket. No bulge. No signalling his intent.

'All right, I'll try it out. You'd better give me some ammunition.'

'No need, it's loaded.'

Andrew turned towards the figure in the tweed jacket, took his time and aimed for the top pocket. There was an explosion and smell of cordite as the bullet removed the lobe of the left ear, and the straw hat floated to the ground.

'Don't shoot him in the face,' yelled Gunther, 'he's our best model.'

'I was aiming at his heart,' snapped Andrew, 'and I am standing fifteen yards away.'

Slowly and deliberately he moved towards the plastic figure whose features gradually assumed the characteristics of Helmut Schmidt. Andrew looked him straight in the eye, and raised the revolver.

'Shoot him in the balls,' giggled the German.

Andrew swung round, furious at the interruption, with the revolver pointing at Gunther.

'No, no, Herr Pringle, don't do it.'

Christ, thought Andrew, what's happening to me? This is obscene, but I'm here and I am going to get it right. 'Keep your mouth shut, Gunther, and let me get on with the job.'

As he turned to face his immobile target there was a faint bleep. The German rushed towards the steel cupboard and picked up a cordless telephone. 'This means trouble, Herr Pringle,' he whispered. 'Keep quiet. Don't make any noise.'

He picked up the receiver and listened. 'Ja', he said several times. Andrew smelt fear emanating from the little man who seemed to be shrinking as he stood there. No more giggling. He was taking orders. But why? And from whom? The shaken man looked at Andrew with fear and hatred in his grey eyes.

'What's up? What's happening?'

'You damn well know what's happening and you can stop using that phoney accent. I thought you were English, but you're not. You've done this to us. You've set us up you bastard.'

'Don't be so bloody crazy. Of course I'm English and I've no idea what you're talking about, so you'd better explain,' said Andrew unconsciously waving the 38 about.

The German wasn't sure any more. The man could be on the level, but the man was holding a gun, and like a fool, because it was the usual practice, he'd put all the others back in the steel cupboard.

'We were followed here. The red Porsche is parked in the farmyard. Speer says there are two men at the back door buying eggs from his wife. He thinks they are police...says that if they find my car hidden away they'll suspect the worst, and start looking for us.'

'Don't be stupid' said Andrew sharply. 'They're not police or intelligence or anything else. No policeman would be allowed to roam the countryside in a vehicle as eye-catching and obvious as a red Porsche.'

Gunther hardly took it in. 'Speer says I'm to get back up and load the car with two small bales of straw, put it in the boot, and drive out alone with the boot open. Make it all look natural and above board. Then, he said, we'll lie low for a few months.'

Andrew thought about his wallet still hidden under the passenger seat. If the two men were undercover agents, and were police, they'd have the right to search the car. They'd find the wallet containing his cheque cards, and he'd be stymied before he started. It had been crass stupidity to book in at the guest house in his own name. Or, he pondered, was Gunther in on it, did he wittingly lead the police to terrorists? Was it all a put-up job? No, he decided, the fear was real enough. In a flash he read the situation with great clarity, quickly making up his mind how to tackle it.

'You are not going anywhere without me,' said Andrew keeping the 38 levelled on the astonished small time arms dealer. 'We're going up on the lift together, but not until you've removed the green shirt and tweed jacket from that obscene target and picked up the straw hat.'

'What do you want them for?'

'I'm going to wear them,' said Andrew remembering the interested expressions on the two men who had walked passed the car with rucksacks on their backs. They'd shown a natural interest, a nod in his direction. Two ramblers out to enjoy themselves who'd noted his white shirt and his grey hair. With the jacket, green shirt, hat to hide his hair, and Gunther's dark glasses, he just might get away with it. He was beginning to enjoy himself.

Gunther wasted no time in disrobing Hermann. He was perky again....saw a way out...put the straw hat on his head and approached Andrew holding out the green shirt and jacket as any well trained valet might do.

'No,' said Andrew tersely. 'Put the clothes on the stool by the safe, stand over there by that red-headed horror, and keep your distance.'

Another inane giggle. 'Don't you trust me?'

'No. Now get back over there.'

Andrew slipped on the green shirt, which was both filthy and foul smelling, over his immaculate white one, while all the time keeping an watchful eye on Gunther. Once he was dressed like the erstwhile model he ordered Gunter to take the lift up and hand over the dark glasses which were in his back pocket.

'They cost me, Herr Pringle, and I need to wear them when I'm driving.'

'You can have them back when we're safely away from this place.'

'You're not coming with me,' squealed the German? Andrew nodded. 'Speer said I was to go it alone. Leave you down here. Said it would be safer.'

'I'll be behind the bales of hay, and at the first sign of any funny business I'll fire this gun which will alert those men.'

Gunther cheered up considerably at the idea of the Englishman being immobilised behind bales of hay. He could deal with that.

Operation Giselle © Teresa Collard 134

'And don't get ideas,' warned Andrew, dreaming up an immediate insurance plan. 'I've posted a letter to my solicitor telling him exactly what I'm doing, where I met you, and the names of your contacts.' It had the desired effect.

'Gott im Himmel,' he whispered, 'why did I think this man was an amateur?'

With the car loaded and the boot lid up Gunther slowly backed out into the farmyard. The two men who were standing by the Porsche talking to Speer looked hard and long at the driver, then more pointedly at the bales of straw. Gunter, with a sickly grin, gave all three men a wave, before driving down the narrow lane. At the end of the lane a weary walker sat on the bank eating an apple. He too took note of the driver and wondered what or who was behind the bales of straw. They turned right on to the main road as Speer's son, driving a tractor, approached from the opposite direction, and turned into the narrow track leading to the farm. The tractor trundled on for a 100 yards effectively blocking a red Porsche which had just emerged from the yard. The farmer's son who was mad on fast cars leapt from his tractor to take a closer look at such perfection. The driver and his passenger were in no mood to talk with enthusiasm about their beast of burden. The boy, no push over, strolled back to his slow moving tractor and waited for them to back into the yard. Strangely enough his engine stalled keeping the impatient men waiting for a further ten minutes, by which time their quarry had vanished.

Gunther had noted both the waiting man and the tractor. He giggled to himself as he weaved through the narrow lanes and farm tracks which he knew like the back of his hand. He could have driven blindfold to the copse where the car would be hidden from the road. It was a bumping bruising ride for the man hidden in the boot of the Volkswagen, but when the car came to a halt he was suddenly afraid. Cocking the gun he held his breath, and waited. A door banged as the driver climbed out of the driving seat, and a few seconds later Andrew heard the familiar giggle as the bales were removed. For once it was a welcome sound.

'Soon have you out of here, Herr Pringle.'

Andrew clambered out slowly, his back aching from the jarring and jolting.

'Where are we?'

'In a wood only a few miles from the farm. We'll have to stay here until it gets dark. There were three men. Two talking to Speer, and one sitting on the verge by the main road watching the exit from the farm.'

'Had he a rucksack with him?'

'Yes.'

'I reckon I saw two of them earlier walking past the car when you were doing your recce. They took a good look at me.'

'That's why you borrowed Hermann's clothes. I'll say this for you Herr Pringle, you're quick for an old one, you're on the ball.'

Andrew pushed the safety catch home, and shoved the gun in his pocket.

'We could complete our business, Herr Pringle, if you're satisfied with the 38?'

'It'll do. There's no going back now. It'll be OK for what I have in mind.'

'Then you owe me a thousand marks, Herr Pringle, which includes the ammunition. If you need more ammo, return to the bar in Koblenz. I'll leave a few rounds with Fritz.'

'There are four rounds left. That's enough,' said Andrew decisively.

The elderly would-be assassin opened the passenger door and slid his arm under the seat and withdrew a battered wallet. The German looked on, flabbergasted. If only he'd known what was under the seat, he could have won the jackpot.

'Thought it was safer to leave it here. Wasn't sure what your set-up was. Didn't intend to be mugged. You see,' said Andrew, laughing at Gunther's expression, 'this is a new experience for me.

A weary man arrived back at St Michael's Gasthaus shortly before midnight. Too tired to eat, too tired to do anything but sleep. His mission accomplished.

Before leaving the hotel Venning made one more phone call praying that Mick Hall would answer. He was in luck. Hearing Mick's rich North Oxfordshire accent was like being home again.

'Good God! A bolt from the blue. What's up, Mr Venning?'

'I have a problem, Mick, which wants solving, like **now**.'

The Inspector didn't remind Mick that he owed him. It was something **neither** man ever mentioned, but Venning had closed his eyes to Mick's harmless hobby. There were plenty who deserved to be in the dock, but not Mick Hall who did more for the community than an army of welfare workers. He ran marathon after marathon raising money for a kidney scanner, cancer research, children in need, and more recently *Aids*.

He'd first met Mick when there'd been a concerted effort to track down pirate radio hams in a forty mile radius of

Birmingham who were putting out pop programmes disregarding Performing Rights, and Phonograph and Mechanical Copyrights. Mick had been a possible suspect. There had been whispers and rumours, but Venning needed incontravertible evidence, and driving home one night through the village of Enstone he'd caught a glimpse of a tell tale aerial being extended on the side of Mick's cottage. Edna Hall opened the door to him, but before she could open her mouth the Inspector was inside, up the stairs, and into the back room. There sat Mick with his headphones on, totally unaware of the policeman standing behind him, talking to a rancher in Texas. Mick, it seemed, hated pop, so they sat down over a pint while he extolled on a hobby which he, and his wife Edna both enjoyed. They'd no children, never likely to have, and this provided them with a consuming interest. They'd contacts all over the world, spent holidays with a lorry driver in Copenhagen, sent flowers when radio-friends were ill, received brochures and letters from hundreds of contacts. There were cases full of the stuff. What amused Venning, at the time, was the idea of a one to one conversation with everyone who cared to listen in, although Mick had stressed that on the outward track only one side of the conversation is heard. On two occasions Mick had been able to assist with cases which had given him a kick. This, thought Venning, would be the third and last time.

'Your present problem, Mr Venning, how can I help?'

'It's a veritable needle in a haystack, Mick, but I need to make immediate contact with an elderly Englishman who is staying either in Trier or Bernkastel. The guy's name is Andrew Pringle.'

'What's he look like?'

'Nearly six foot, thick grey hair, dark blue eyes, extremely agile, speaks German fluently, and is an ex-RAF pilot who, after the war, worked in Local Government. I want to know where he is, but softly, softly. If he is traced I don't want him to know we're on to him.'

'Got it, Mr Venning. Bernkastel is a doddle. I have a contact there, a Jacob Misch who's a wine grower with a son who runs a small delicatessen in Bernkastel. Dieter, who is in his early thirties, also chats over the waves. Can't help you with Trier. Don't know anyone there, but I daresay Jacob will help out. I'm sure he'll come up with something.

'You're the tops, Mick. I don't know how you do it.'

'And where, Mr Venning, can I contact you?'

'That's the sixty four thousand dollar question, Mick, but I'll ring you later tonight when I've found somewhere to lay my head.'

Inspector Venning booked in at the Haus Constanze in Kues. It was ideally placed, with a panoramic view from his bedroom balcony and only ten minutes on foot to Bernkastel on the east bank of the Moselle. Before making tracks he rang Mick Hall. 'Any luck, Mick?'

'Yes and no. Neither Jacob nor Dieter remember seeing anyone answering to your father-in-law's description, but that's because they weren't looking for him.'

Venning laughed. 'I know what you mean.'

'But Dieter would like to meet you, get a fuller description, look at a photograph, and then he'll see what he can do.'

'Excellent!'

'Dieter says it will enliven his dreary predictable routine. Says he can always leave his wife in charge of the shop. Do you want me to tell him where you're staying?'

'A good idea. We can have a chat over a glass of wine and the sooner the better. Tell him I'm staying at the Haus Constanze in Kues, and I'll expect him at any time after 1900 hours.'

'OK, and there's another thing, Mr Venning.'

'Yes?'

'He says there are hundreds of apartments, flats, guest houses and hotels in Bernkastel, Kues, Andel and Wehlen, the four small townships which all abut the river.'

'Are you saying he thinks it's a hopeless task?'

'Only if the elderly man with a mop of grey hair is wearing a hat!'

'You're a pessimist, Mick. Think positive, and thanks for everything, Mick. I'll not be worrying you again, ever.'

'Don't say that, Mr Venning. I enjoy the challenge.'

One more call before his pre-dinner constitutional. Joyce sounded more cheerful. 'You said the world was a large place, Julian.'

'I did, but fortunately our world has shrunk. All happening, if we're lucky, within a five mile radius.'

'When you find him, tell him we love him, tell him we miss him, and tell him to come home.'

'Your father, my love, is the most single-minded person who's ever crossed my path, and I doubt whether he'll listen to me, but I'll talk to him, try to make him see reason.'

'If he won't,' said Joyce nervously, will you, will you...'

'Inform the authorities? No. It's a problem I'll have to solve myself.'

She sighed. 'I feel helpless here, and I'd be a burden to you there.'

'You're invaluable where you are. If you receive another card or if he rings you get in touch immediately. The code is 06531, and the number 6708. If I'm out leave a message.'

As Venning replaced the phone he wondered whether ex-pilot Oberleutnant Schmidt lived alone, or was he already cold, lying undiscovered, in his own home? He'd get over straight away. Buy a map and make his way to Burgstrasse.

EIGHT

Helmut Schmidt hummed softly to himself as he placed the crockery and cutlery in the dishwasher. Much easier to wash them by hand, he thought to himself. Why did his daughter Josepha always insist that in the interests of hygiene the machine must be used? But he did draw the line at allowing the brute to grind the two small egg cups to pulp. As usual he washed them lovingly. Only two left now of the six his wife had bought for her bottom drawer three days after their engagement. Ingrid wouldn't have agreed to the dishwasher being installed, but Ingrid had been a Hausfrau, happy in her home, not a get-up-and-go business woman like her daughter.

Ingrid's death from *carcinoma uteri* six years previously had left him with little will to live. The light had gone out of his life. No fun any more. No dashing out and doing things on the spur of the moment. Josepha moved in with him and changed all that.

'You must get out and do things, father. Have a regular routine. Stop having the paper delivered. Walk down into the town and pick one up. Cross the bridge, take a stroll along the river each day. Have a coffee near the Weinmuseum. On Tuesdays wet or fine take the river cruise up to Traben Trarbach and back. Always have your lunch in town.'

When he argued about the unnecessary expense she was blunt as only a hard headed business woman can be.

'You need company. Do you want to die, a lonely old man, sitting in your armchair all day? I don't want to be worrying about you, father. I want to know when I'm away on business that you're eating properly which elderly people rarely do if they're left on their own.'

Josepha's advice had made good sense, but what she didn't seem to realise was that his arthritis made moving around a hilly town like Bernkastel far from easy, but he loved Bernkastel, and there he would stay. Sometimes he walked down to St Michael's Gasthaus, and sometimes when the weather was good and he was feeling more buoyant he would eat at St Sebastian's cafe at the bottom of the road. His favourite dish was Strammer Max, which was both reasonable and filling, and all for 11 marks. Two pieces of bread covered in quantities of ham, always too much ham, and on top of that two fried eggs. At his age it was more than he really needed.

Helmut wasn't allowed to drive any more, his swollen hip joint had put paid to that, but again Josepha came up with an answer.

'You can't expect your old friends at the Landrat to come over here, so take a taxi, go into the office and have a chat. Take a glass of wine with them after work. It will give you an interest.'

Josepha was too much of a high flier, thought Helmut. She'd no idea how short people's memories were, and why, simply because you'd worked with them, would they want to see you again? Most of his close colleagues in the legal department had long since retired, very few remaining in Wittlich. The employees now in the office were younger men and women, all eager to get straight home at the end of the day to their families. Not one of them would want to give up precious time talking to a fuddy-duddy with no interests. No one. Not now.

Ingrid, beloved Ingrid, had been too concerned with his pain to notice her own. She'd read everything relating to arthritis that she could lay her hands on. He'd tried all the diets and ideas she'd come up with. They'd spent weeks taking a tablespoon of cider vinegar, and a tablespoonful of honey before each meal. Ingrid didn't have to take the stuff but she liked to keep him company. It was a cure, Ingrid had explained, that a cattle farmer in the United States had chanced upon. He'd become accustomed to the sight of his cows limping round the field, all suffering the effects of arthritis, until one day he couldn't believe his eyes. They all looked more robust, were moving more easily. The improvement was inexplicable until he discovered they'd been drinking cider from large vats tucked away in a corner of his barn. The milk yield may have been a little thinner, but the cows mooed and moved more happily in their bovine way.

    The cider-honey treatment did nothing for Helmut's arthritis, but it certainly caused Ingrid to lose weight, or that's what they thought at the time. The next experiment was to cut out coffee and drink weak tea. Thankfully Ingrid didn't expect him to give up his favourite tipple, a dry Urziger, despatched monthly from the vineyard at Urzig. Cutting out coffee did help a little, inasmuch as they both slept a great deal better. And then finally Ingrid came up with a diet that did work. No red meat, no oranges, lemons, grapefruit or tomatoes, and again no coffee. It was miraculous. Helmut began moving about again like a young man, Stairs were no trouble, driving the car posed no problem, he could weed without having to kneel, and he no longer relied on his walking stick. He was rejuvenated. Ingrid, happy to see the change, decided she'd better do something about a constant pain which she'd endured for more than a year.

It was too late. Far, far too late.

    Two months after Ingrid's death Josepha moved in with her father. She didn't sell her flat in Koblenz because she knew that one day she'd move back again, permanently. Life in Bernkastel Kues would never suit her. Far too parochial for her lifestyle. She loved Koblenz, everything about it, especially her job as a Director of a Public Relations firm, with a branch in the city, whose clients were owners of vineyards all needing to have their produce put on the international map. It was a job she'd landed on her thirty fifth birthday. Two days later she took possession of a flat in an eighteenth century building in Kastorhof. The view was something she'd never give up, not even for her father. From time to time she returned to sit on the balcony and gaze down on the *Deutsches Eck*, a vast imperial monument at the confluence of the Rhine and Moselle; from the flat she could marvel at the hilltop Fortress of Ehrenbreitstein on the south bank of the Rhine, and immediately opposite the flat stood St Kastor's church a stunning Romanesque edifice which provided her with the only spiritual uplift she was ever likely to experience because she never ventured inside.

It was a damp day, excellent for the vines on the hillside behind the house, but cruel for any man or beast suffering from arthritis. Helmut locked the front door of his home in Burgstrasse and walked slowly, painfully, down into the town. Why couldn't he get rid of this niggling thought? No, it was more than that, it was disturbing, something he should have discussed with Josepha, but she'd have laughed her head off, told him not to be an old fool and to take a little less of the vino. She might have said all that, but her face would have reflected her thoughts. Senile dementia his daughter would have been thinking--no, he daren't say a word. Supposing, and the thought terrified him, supposing she was right? The idea was more frightening than anything he'd had to face in 72 years. Perhaps it was time to dig out those tablets he'd hidden away after Ingrid's death? Pethadine, which the medic had prescribed to kill pain, but that was five years ago. Did they lose their efficacy, and if they did were there enough left to finish the business? The Dutch, he mused, had the right approach, maybe a nursing home in Amsterdam was the answer? It would be quick, dignified, not messy. No enquiries, no inquest, no loose ends for his daughter to worry about. Was that why Josepha hadn't sold her flat? Had she recognised the symptoms of senility, Altzeimer's disease, they called it, and had she discussed it with his doctor? Perhaps she'd decided to sell the house once he was committed to one of those hideous places for the old and mentally defective? No, he daren't mention his problem, daren't say a word, it would be tantamount to admitting his mind was going.

He stopped half way down Römerstrasse and came to a decision. If he was being followed there was only one way to find out. Lead the fellow a dance, get him into a situation where they had to come face to face. His hip was more painful then usual, and the new cobblestones more slippery. Everywhere he walked these days there were men at work replacing the old cobbles in readiness for the town's 700 year celebration in 1991. It would be slow progress crossing the bridge, but not so easy for the man following him to hide. He'd lead him along by the river to the Weinmuseum. He had to prove to himself that he was not hallucinating, that he was as sane as the next man. He stopped at the bottom of the street to pick up his paper, looked round to see if he was being followed, but there was no sign of the man who was beginning to haunt him. Helmut made his way to the cafe in the square where he sat in his accustomed place in the window and waited for Ulrike to bring his coffee. The news looked the same every morning, man destroying man in every quarter of the globe. And now another maniac had emerged. This time in the Gulf. When would it ever stop? He held the newspaper slightly below his eye level and peered into the square. Tourists were already gathering to gaze at the half-timbered fairy tale houses built in the 16th century, and at the flamboyant figure of St Michael atop his fountain. Good God! There was the man, standing in front of the Rathaus, it didn't make sense, it...

'Your coffee, Herr Schmidt.'

'Thank you, Ulrike, thank you.'

For a second he was diverted, and when he looked again the familiar figure, of a tall lean man with a shock of grey hair, had vanished.

The man with the shock of grey hair had stayed for a few days at the Hotel Behrens in Schanzstrasse. A bed and breakfast hotel with main meals available at the Altes Brauhaus 600 metres down the road. They'd given him a comfortable room with a balcony overlooking the Moselle, perfect for a peaceful tranquil holiday. Large barges, heavy with containers, and many of them flying the Dutch flag, moved slowly up and down the river, never competing with faster pleasure cruisers. But he wasn't on holiday, this man with the grey hair. He'd been doing his homework and after three days in the hotel he moved to St Michael's Gasthaus at the corner of Hinterm Graben and Kallenfelsstrasse.

For Andrew Pringle the few sentences he'd read in the Luftwaffe Reference Library in Freiburg recording Schmidt's desire to work in the Rathaus in Wittlich, once hostilities were over, gave him all the information he needed. He had wasted no time, arrived in Wittlich the following day and hung around outside the modern, but elegant, local government offices which stood four square in the centre of town, waiting for the staff to leave. Only two men, both middle aged, made their way to the local Bierkeller. He waited until they'd downed a couple of steins before approaching them, buying a round, and congratulating them on their wonderful sports facilities, especially their tennis school. Quite casually he mentioned Helmut Schmidt, an old acquaintance. Was he alive and kicking? Did he still live in the area, and what about his family? The Germans didn't seem particularly interested in Helmut, hadn't seen him since his retirement some ten years before, but they knew his wife had died, and they knew he was still living across the river in Bernkastel. In a house, Andrew discovered, which stood alongside a graveyard and small church in Burgstrasse.

For days he'd followed Schmidt, knew the time he left home, knew the latch on his garden gate at the side of his house was faulty, knew the time he picked up his newspaper, where he had coffee, the day on which he took his river trip, and the restaurants he frequented, sometimes St Sebastian, and sometimes St Michael's Gasthaus. Helmut Schmidt was unaware that the man who perpetually dogged his foorsteps was staying at the gasthaus where he lunched.

Andrew stood, motionless, some distance from the river, watched his quarry walk slowly over the bridge towards Kues and waited until Schmidt was almost across before tacking himself on to a voluble party of sightseers. Helmut, who was intent on visiting the Weinmuseum turned right at the end of the bridge, but the effort had exhausted him. He was tired, and dispirited. It was all proving too much. He changed his mind, decided to visit the Cusanus Convent, it wasn't quite as far. He could sit in the chapel, take the weight off his feet, that was easy enough, but could he take the weight off his mind?

The tourists also turned right and Andrew with them. He listened to the one woman who seemed to know it all.

'The convent we're visiting,' she told her party, 'which is 500 years old, is a hospital dedicated to Cardinal Nicholaus von Kues, a 15th century scholar and philosopher who was born here. Your visit would be incomplete without learning something about this great man.'

'When are we going to do the wine tasting?' piped up an acne covered youth.

'Late this afternoon,' snapped the woman. 'You had more than was good for you last night.'

'Count me out, Mrs Gellard. I'm going to sit by the river.'

'Don't you want to see the Gutenberg Bible?'

'The Guten what?'

Mrs Gellard gave up.

Andrew was sweating profusely. It was a hot humid day, too hot for a jacket, but how else could he carry a gun? Schmidt who was only a few yards ahead entered the building. The pain was excruciating, but not in vain because the man who had been shadowing him for days was close behind. The Gothic chapel, a blissfully peaceful place, was empty. Helmut sat on the front pew, as he always did, it gave him space to stretch his right leg. Perhaps he should have had the hip replacement Josepha was always nagging about? But why bother, he'd nothing left to live for? As he relaxed the pain subsided and he found himself absorbed in the altar triptych. Why had he never noticed before how cleverly the artist had balanced the colours in the central panel? The mother of Jesus, the only figure in black, and beside her in red stood St John comforting her. On the right side were two figures on horseback dressed in muted red garments, but his eye went naturally to the three crosses with Christ in the centre. Despite his concentration he heard a slight sound as a door behind him opened. He was no longer alone. There was no need to turn, his sixth sense told him that a grey haired man had just entered the chapel.

For some seconds Andrew stood looking at the back of a man who had no idea how close he was to death. It was an ideal place. The body would fall in front of the seats, and not be immediately visible from the door, giving him time to get away and mingle with the tourists, but there'd be no time to face Schmidt, tell him why he had to die. No, I can't do it that way. I owe you, Peter. He has to know. Quietly the man whose heart was full of hate left the chapel.

For Helmut those quiet moments had not been wasted. Josepha was always saying the Lord worked in mysterious ways. How did she know this daughter of his who claimed to be a non-believer? But she was right. He'd deal with the problem. Put his mind at rest.

To his joy, Andrew found the resplendent Gothic Library was full of ancient books, many handwritten, illuminated, leather bound, and centuries old. He was concentrating on a section of books written in the 15th century by Nicholaus von Kues. His Latin was rusty, all he could remember was amar, amo, amat, and perhaps that wasn't right! What did *De concordantia catholica* mean exactly? Catholic harmony, perhaps?

'A splendid book,' said the man beside him. He turned and gazed into expressionless blue eyes.

'Yes,' said Andrew taken aback. 'I was...I was wondering what it was all about.'

The man's voice was deep, deeper than he'd imagined. 'Nicholaus was 500 years ahead of his time, and obsessed with preserving Church Unity. He also felt strongly that the General Council should be more democratic reflecting the views of the faithful, and the Pope should adopt the role of an administrative Primate.'

'He didn't win, though, did he?' said Andrew quickly.

'No, but he didn't lose either, because he changed his ideas and became the Pope's champion.'

Andrew laughed derisively. 'We all change our ideas, but the Church is riddled with politics, both Catholic and Anglican.'

'Ah, you are English, Mr...?'

'Pringle. Andrew Pringle.'

Damn, thought Andrew. This man is using the same tactics he used 45 years ago. Infiltrate, get in close, and attack. This time, however, he's made a mistake, and so have I. He damn well knows I'm following him.

'It's strange,' said Andrew, thinking that attack was better then defence, 'I've seen you around quite a bit, but always on the other side of the Moselle.'

'Yes, you will have done, because that's where I live. But what are you doing in Bernkastel Herr Pringle?'

Here we go again, thought Andrew. He's taking the initiative. 'I'm spending a long holiday going where the mood takes me.'

'And the mood has deposited you in Bernkastel?'

'Yes.'

'Most people find a week gives them sufficient time for sightseeing.'

But it's not long enough, thought Andrew, to do the job thoroughly. Helmut glanced at the ring on the Englishman's finger.

'Is your wife with you Herr Pringle?'

'My wife is dead.'

'Forgive me. I'm sorry. So is mine,' he added softly. 'Don't you find it ironic, Herr Pringle, that we're both here in the right surroundings?'

'What do you mean?'

'Nicholaus Krebs or Krues as we know him now established this hospital for the care of 33 needy men over the age of 50.'

'Why 33?'

'One for each year of Christ's life. It's still functioning today in exactly the way Nicholaus intended.'

'That explains the 18th century paintings depicting acts of charity.'

'Yes. Food for the hungry, clothing for the naked, freedom for the imprisoned, visitors for the sick, shelter for the stranger and burial for the dead.'

Was it his imagination, was he becoming ultra-sensitive wondered Andrew, or had the German laid more stress on shelter for the stranger, and burial for the dead? What the hell was he doing? The last thing he needed was dialogue with this man. 'Krebs,' he said suddenly, 'does the word, Herr Schmidt, mean crayfish?'

The German was startled. What is this man, who knows my name, doing here?

'Oh yes, it means crayfish, that is why the sign is on the coat of arms.'

Andrew knew he'd been careless, couldn't quite bring himself to look into those searching blue eyes. Helmut Schmidt felt the unease, recognised that his companion was on edge. But why? His curiosity was aroused. Not knowing provided a brief interest to enlighten the days that carried him so slowly towards his end.

As they left the building Helmut asked Andrew whether he'd ever taken the river trip from Bernkastel to Traben-Trarbach. If not would he care to accompany him the following day?

Andrew hesitated, then a brilliant idea flashed through his mind.

'I could prove to be an excellent guide, point out all the vineyards, the bridges and the ruined castles. Do join me.'

'Thankyou, Herr Schmidt. I'll take you up on your offer. What time do we leave?

'The boat departs from Bernkastel at 10.00 and arrives at Traben-Trarbach at 11.50. We could have a snack lunch and catch the boat back at 13.30.'

One thing you won't be doing, thought Andrew, is catch the boat back.

NINE

There were advantages, mused Andrew, in being lame as he watched the chatting knots of holiday makers unravel as Helmut Schmidt approached the *Brünhilde*, and boarded her without first having to queue. Andrew didn't hurry. There was no need, he knew Schmidt would reserve a seat for him. Instead he surveyed the boat. Larger than he expected. The lower deck almost totally under cover. A few seats in the bows, but far too public for what he had in mind. The upper deck, on which the bridge was situated, was only partially covered. Again some seats in the bows where passengers were already seated, and plenty in the stern where the house flag drooped, its colours hardly distinguishable. No breeze, a close humid still day, an ominous stillness. A stillness which presaged disaster.

Andrew boarded with the final group of passengers, who were all in their mid-fifties, all French, all talking and no one listening, but he had to hand it to them, they were lively vivacious and strenuously making every effort to enjoy their *vacances.* The gangplank was removed, the painters retrieved, and *Brünhilde* was under way. Almost immediately a voice came over the loudspeakers welcoming them aboard. A polyglot in French, German, English and Italian, who then proceeded with instructions on how to abandon ship should a crisis occur. Passengers hardly listened to the warning, but were far more attentive when it came to bar and buffet facilities. A coffee would be welcome but first of all he'd take a look at the upper deck. He found it crowded, as he'd expected, but those damned irremovable seats fixed all round the perimeter of the open area were an obstacle to his planning.

There was little room for manoeuvre, the only available space was alongside the flagpole in the stern.

"Don't do it, don't think about it." He turned round, but there was no one beside him. How could there be? Emily's voice had been clear enough. She was still with him. Wouldn't let him be.

"Andrew, listen to me." He was with her now in the garden. "Can't you understand, Andrew, that you're destroying yourself? You are letting an unknown German cause you unbelievable mental distress. Lingering and painful, far worse than anything Peter experienced. Peter was free of this world in a few seconds, and now he is at peace, so too, I hope to God, is that poor German. Forget him, Andrew, he was only doing his job."

'Only!'

"Why don't you make an effort, Andrew to find peace? Talk to Dr Fletcher, if it will help. He is a most compassionate and understanding man."

'No one can help me, Emily. Stop suggesting it's an illness. It isn't. I am keeping faith with Peter. You surely don't expect me to break my word?'

"Do you really think Peter would have wanted you to self-destruct?"

His reverie was disturbed by a further announcement.

'Would Herr Pringle please go to the coffee bar where Herr Schmidt is waiting for him.'

Damnnation, here we go again, thought Andrew. The first strike, as usual.

Helmet looked up with a slight smile on his face. 'Do sit down, my friend. Thought I'd lost you, but the staff on the *Brünhilde* are always so obliging. They offered to call you.'

'Always! Do you make this trip very often?'

'Yes, every week.' The Englishman's surprise was real. Why didn't he know about these trips? He's been following me for ten days. Must have known what I was doing last week. Dear God, am I really senile? Is it all in my mind?

'Do they reserve this table for you every week?'

'Yes.'

'Then you are spoilt, Herr Schmidt.'

'This trip is one of my daughter Josepha's better ideas. She suggested a weekly outing would do me good. Get her old father out of the house. Always has to manage people, does my daughter, but for once she was right. You'll see what I mean. She's meeting us in Traben for lunch.'

Damn, damn, damn. That's an added complication.

'Does your daughter live with you, Herr Schmidt?'

'Yes she does. Herr Pringle,' said Helmut as he absent mindedly added a second cube of sugar to his coffee. I think you should call me Helmut? Protocol is rather unnecessary at our great age. And you, I'm sure will have no objection to me addressing you as Andrew?'

Why does this man always take the iniative? 'Yes, yes, that's OK with me.'

'Do you have any children, Andrew?'

'Yes, one daughter. She's married, happily married.'

'We're two of a kind. Widowers, each with one daughter. Each with time to kill. And, just to satisfy my curiosity, what sort of profession did you follow?'

It wasn't idle curiosity, it was a dimly conscious idea that didn't quite filter through. There was something amiss. But what?

'My job!' Andrew laughed. 'It was nothing very memorable. A job which provided occasional interest, but the boredom heavily outweighed the odd occurrences which stretched my mind. I actually spent 40 years in a profoundly boring Local Government post.'

'Good God,' Helmut roared. 'I don't believe this. I too worked in Local Government, the Rathaus at Wittlich. Fortunately, unlike you, I found it interesting.'

Helmut waved at the young blonde waitress.

'More coffee, Herr Schmidt?' she shouted. He nodded.

'I'll be with you in a moment.'

While Helmut waited for the coffee Inspector Julian Venning was half way through a late, late breakfast. He'd already covered hotels and gasthauses on the the west side of Kues, thinking the early morning the best time to catch Andrew. Browsing through a paper, enjoying the peace, and the spectacular view of the mountains on the other side of the valley. Truly an idyllic spot, but he couldn't linger too long, he had to cover the rest of Kues. Dieter, he knew, was systematically phoning all the hotels and gasthauses in Bernkastel before embarking on the flats and apartments. Suddenly his view of the mountains was totally blocked by a tall thin man standing in front of the table.

'Are you Inspector Venning, sir?'

'Yes.'

'May I join you?' The stranger didn't wait for an answer, but sat. Venning took in the fellow at a glance. A lean sinewy man dressed in a blue T shirt, and fawn slacks. Fit, intelligent, about 30, mousey hair, hazel eyes, unattractive, but determined.

'You are an army officer, I take it? said Venning.

'Yes, sir. Group Captain Dadswell told me to report. Give you the low down to date. I am Jonathan Neal, a lieutenant with Military Intelligence. He handed over his identity card. Venning looked at it briefly before passing it back.

'Well Lieutenant, you'd better get on with it.'

'We've lost Pringle, sir.'

'You what!' Venning was furious. 'You lost him! Do you mean that Group Captain Dadswell has initiated this operation without reference to me?'

'Yes, sir.'

'It would have helped, Lieutenant, if you'd had the courtesy to put me in the picture.'

'Group thought it might be preferable if we picked him up, less embarrassing for you, sir.'

'What does that mean?'

'Arresting your father-in-law wouldn't be quite the thing, sir.'

'I've no intention of arresting him. I'm going to find him and take him home. And now you're here, Lieutenant, you'd better tell me where he's staying.'

'We don't know, sir. We've kept a watch on Kastelhaus, Schmidt's house, which is the only lead we had, and we saw Pringle following the German. Difficult to pick him up, too public, we had to bide our time. Half an hour later we saw the subject board a bus for Trier, which we followed. He then made tracks for the Roman amphitheatre. We were about to take him when he was joined by a German. The two of them left the arena and made their way to MacDonalds. We didn't want to cause a scene so we sat in the car and waited.'

'How many of you?'

'Three including Jock who knows Trier well. Half an hour later the two men left in a clapped out V.W, and we followed in a Porsche.'

Venning spluttered, hastily wiping his mouth with a napkin. 'You followed in a Porsche! One of the most noticeable and elegant cars on the road.'

'It's Group's, sir. He said to take it, thinking we wouldn't look like military police in something so flamboyant.'

'Well, Lieutenant, you followed. What then?'

'We lost him, sir. We know where he went, and what he was doing, but we lost him.'

'Where did they go?' asked Venning knowing he would have panned his sergeant for being so careless.

'They drove to a farm and parked the car in one of the stables. Two of my men saw Pringle go in, but they didn't see him leave as such.'

'What on earth does 'as such' mean?'

'The Volkswagen left with straw bales in the boot. We think Pringle was under them.'

'And the speedy Porsche was no match for the VW? Is that it?'

'We were blocked by a tractor in a narrow lane. Intentionally, I would have said.'

Venning laughed.

'What's so funny, sir?' Lieutenant Neal was annoyed.

'My 70 year old father-in-law taking you fellows for a ride both literally and metaphorically. Now, Lieutenant, you'd better tell me what they were doing at the farm.'

'We're almost certain he was buying a fire-arm. The German Police have had the farm under surveillance for weeks, but haven't been able to nail anyone.

Christ, thought Venning. I'm too late. My father-in-law at large, with a gun.

All I can do now is pray.

Fräulein Thiesen bustled in. 'There's a call for you, Herr Venning, in reception.'

He was out of his chair and into reception in one flowing movement.

'Yes?'

'Come quickly, Herr Venning. I've found him.'

Venning replaced the phone and found Fräulein Thiesen standing beside him.

'Fräulein, please serve the gentleman at my table with a jug of fresh coffee.'

'Certainly Herr Venning.'

That will keep him occupied, thought the Inspector happily.

As he left the gasthaus he looked for a Porsche. Good God, it was red. Crass stupidity! The two men in the car had their eyes fixed on the door. They watched him as he went into the garden, no idea he was an English policeman, unaware too that he'd decided not to use his hired car, but to walk over the bridge, and leave them twiddling their thumbs. Parking in Bernkastel was always a hazard. In the event he ran over the bridge, across the square, and up the hill to the delicatessen. Dieter was serving a customer. He waited. It gave him just enough time to get his breath back.

Dieter's exuberance was infectious. 'Your search is nearly at an end, my friend. When Herr Pringle first arrived in Bernkastel he stayed at the Hotel Behrens for three days before moving to St Michael's Gasthaus where he's been for some time. It's not far Herr Venning.'

'How far?'

'Out of here, along Römerstrasse which brings you to Hinterm Graben. Cross the road and you'll find St Michael's on the corner.'

'Many thanks, Dieter. Couldn't have done this without you.'

'I've enjoyed it, Herr Venning.

The day was too hot and too humid for rushing about. He wiped his hands and his forehead before entering the Gasthaus, but there was nothing he could do about his saturated shirt. He rang the bell in reception and waited impatiently for someone to attend the desk.

'Good day, sir. What can I do for you? asked a young lad with a grin which stretched from ear to ear. It was his first job. His first morning.

'I'd like to speak to Herr Pringle who is staying here.'

'Herr Pringle? Is he the English gentleman?'

'Yes, the elderly Englishman with the grey hair.'

'He went out, sir, about an hour ago.'

'Do you know where he went?'

'No. Sorry, sir, he didn't say.

'Thanks son, thanks. I'll sit down for a moment and think.' Venning didn't sit. He collapsed into an armchair.

Fresh coffee arrived and the *Brünhilde* sailed on and on. Andrew knew he was becoming decidedly edgy. 'Do you remain in this coffee bar?' Andrew still couldn't bring himself to say *Helmut*. 'Do you stay here throughout the voyage?'

'No, but I find on cold days that it's warm, and on hot days it's cool. Not only that, since Ingrid died I've become a coffee addict. Does my arthritis no good, but I might as well enjoy what I can while I can.'

'Anyone would think, hearing you talk, that you're expecting to die at any moment.'

'Today or tomorrow, what does it matter? I've had enough. Life without Ingrid is no fun any more, and each day I find the physical struggle almost insurmountable. Don't get me wrong, Andrew, I'm not feeling sorry for myself, I've just had enough.' Just as well, thought Andrew, because I mean to help you on your way.

'Haven't you thought about having a hip replacements? he asked in an almost caring and civilised manner.

'I'm not allowed to forget. Josepha nags me silly about having both hips operated on, but don't you see, I'd be totally dependent on her for weeks, maybe months. Bernkastel isn't the place for a man on crutches, so she'd have to fetch and carry. I saw enough of people on crutches during the war, saw the sympathy the damned sticks engendered. Mind you there were some notable exceptions like Bader, that English pilot, who never needed sympathy, who lost both legs and still managed to command a squadron.'

'Not for long,' said Andrew quickly. 'He was captured in 1941, but you couldn't keep him down could you? He caused more mayhem on the ground than he'd ever caused in the air. Kept your men on their toes, and escaped, God alone knows how, many times.'

'A remarkable man,' smiled Helmut, 'whose attributes became all the more astonishing in wartime. I wish I'd known him.'

Andrew was about to admit he'd met Bader when he was training in Canada, but quickly shut his mouth.

'Which service were you in Andrew?'

At that moment fresh coffee and biscuits arrived, and Andrew hurriedly changed the subject.

'Tell me...tell me...Helmut' He had difficulty in mouthing the name, what are those villages on the right bank, the two with the steepled churches?'

'Ah, the first village is Zeltingen, it has a pretty church well worth a visit, and the one on the bend is Rachtig, and as soon as we get round the curve of the river I'll show you the most important place in the district, the most important for me, anyway.'

Helmut poured two coffees. 'Help yourself to milk and sugar.'

'Just milk,' said Andrew as he poured it in liberally to weaken the strong coffee. 'Don't you ever wander round the boat, go aloft once in a while to enjoy the view?'

'Yes. I usually go on deck during the return journey which is no more of a struggle than walking up Burgstrasse.'

As soon as the *Brünhilde* passed under the bridge which served Zeltingen and Rachtig Helmut pointed to vine covered hills on the left bank. 'That my friend is Urzig where my favourite wine's produced. I get through a case a week much to Josepha's consternation. You must join me one night. We'll enjoy a convivial evening together.'

Helmut wondered why his invitation, had in some way, disturbed the Englishman. There was something odd, something he couldn't put his finger on.

'Excuse me,' said Andrew abruptly, 'I'll take a walk on the upper deck.' He didn't need a walk. He needed air, space in which to think clearly. Earlier that morning as he lay in the bath it had all seemed so easy, so straightforward. Now he wasn't sure. He was slowly becoming enmeshed in Schmidt's daily problems, the bossy daughter, arthritis, his addiction to coffee and wine, and now an invitation to share it with him. For his present plan he didn't need the gun. It was safely hidden, he'd secreted it, like criminals do, in the lavatory cistern, securely wrapped and fastened in plastic bags. A slight push and it would all be over. It would have to happen on the way back. The only pity, there'd be no time to tell him why.

He was standing by the flagpole looking at the limp flag when a sudden gust of wind lifted it aloft displaying, for all to see, a blue anchor emblazoned on a cream background. *Brünhilde* was midstream sailing round the second large bend, with Traben in sight, when a second more forceful gust shook the boat.

'My goodness,' said the person at his side who was gripping the taffrail, 'just look at the swell.'

Andrew didn't look at the swell, he stared in amazement at Helmut.

For a split second the German saw undisguised hatred in the Englishman's eyes which quickly changed to concern and astonishment. Was this man crazy, wondered Andrew? Hadn't he felt the vibes? Had he no idea that his days, maybe even minutes were numbered? Why struggle up the steps? Had he a death wish? Did he want to die?

The sky was blue and cloudless, but the gusts became more violent. Now was the time. How fate had played into his hands. Two small yachts were in trouble, being buffeted about by a swirling wind. No one was looking at him. Everyone was intent on the yachtsmen who were reefing in the sails, and fighting desperately to avoid being swept full pelt against the right bank. He put his hand on Helmut's shoulder.

'Don't worry about me, Andrew, you look after yourself.'

'Herr Schmidt, Herr Schmidt,' yelled a crew member as he rushed up the steps. 'Hang on, sir, hang on. We'll get you back down again.'

'Don't worry, Jan, my friend will help me.'

'Damnation,' said Andrew softly as he let go of Helmut. The sailor ignoring Helmut's protestations gave him a hand as he descended the steep steps to the lower deck. Damn the man. It could all have been over. Andrew swearing at his bad luck reluctantly returned to the coffee bar, and sat down at the corner table.

Brünhilde received another violent onslaught which the master steadied by turning into the wind. There were no longer any passengers sitting in the uncovered areas, neither were they walking the decks any more. The Master advised them to remain seated and stay under cover, also warning them that high winds would make it impossible for him to tie up in Traben.

The two men looked on in horror as one of the small yachts capsized and spewed three life jacketed men into the river who, miraculously, managed to hang on to the upturned keel. Within moments a police launch came into view. It too was thrown around like a cork, unable to make contact or get anywhere near the unfortunate men. For a few seconds the whirlwind abated and during the lull the police fired a maroon, with a rope attached, at the keel of the yacht. Helmut leant forward to get a better view, and at that moment *Brünhilde* made a 90 degreee turn which made it impossible to watch the outcome of the rescue.

'Poor devils,' said Helmut. A hellish situation. I wonder what they're thinking about? One reads so often that in moments

before death ones whole life passes before us. Do you believe it, Andrew, or is it an old wive's tale?'
Andrew didn't look at Helmut, his reply barely audible. 'I hope with all my heart it's true.'

Venning sighed as he watched the boy with the ecstatic grin return to the kitchen. The boy told Fraulein Jurgens about the man who had flopped into an armchair in the foyer; about the man who so desperately wanted to talk to Herr Pringle. Fräulein Jürgens had a shrewd idea where her guest was bound. She hurried into the foyer.

'Herr Venning, is your business with Herr Pringle urgent?'

'Yes, it's a family matter that can't wait. Have you any idea where he is?'

'Herr Pringle never said anything, you understand, but at breakfast I noticed him studying a time table. The blue one that covers Bernkastel to Traben Trarbach.'

'Wonderful, Fraulein. Perhaps you could direct me to the bus station?'

She laughed. 'If he's gone to Traben, he's gone by boat.'

'Boat!' echoed Venning. So what time did he leave?'

'In plenty of time to catch the 10 o'clock. The journey takes two hours so he should be there by noon. He might disembark, have lunch which many people do, and catch the 1.30 back.'

'Which means he could be back here at the Gasthaus by 4 o'clock?

'Yes, that's right.'

'Thank you Fräulein, you've been most helpful. I'll be back here in time for a cup of tea.'

Why on earth, wondered Venning, as he made his way to Kastelhaus in Burgstrasse, was Andrew taking a pleasure trip up the river? So far everything he's done has led directly to Schmidt's demise. How does a boat trip fit into the scheme of things? Venning rejected the idea of returning to Haus Constanze, picking up the car and driving to Traben. He might just make it, get there ahead of the boat, but Andrew could have disembarked anywhere en route. No that wasn't the answer. He'd take a look at Schmidt's house, make sure he was still alive, and then go down to the landing stage and wait. There was a sudden gust of wind causing a cyclist to waver alarmingly in the middle of the road. By the time he'd straightened up there was another tremendous blast. The man gave up the unequal struggle, dismounted, and pushed the bike along the path ahead of the Inspector. As they both rounded the curve in the road Venning was not surprised to see a red Porsche parked alongside the church. Dadswell's men were casing Kastelhaus. He caught a sudden reflection, someone with binoculars was standing in front of the castle on top of the hill facing the front of Schmidt's house.

The storm ceased as abruptly as it had begun. The Master of the *Brünhilde* warned passengers that he could no longer stick to the schedule. All boats would be running at least an hour late.

'Thank God, Andrew, that time doesn't worry us any more. Look!' he said suddenly, 'there's Josepha standing on the quay waiting for us.'

A soon as the two men stepped on terra firma they found themselves being organised.

'I've booked lunch for three at the hostellerie in Zel. We'll go in my car,' said Josepha.

'But,' protested Helmut, 'I prefer a cheap lunch here.'

'That's no way to treat a visitor, ' said Josepha firmly, 'and not only that I have a problem we have to share. Something that can't wait.'

As Andrew sipped his beetroot soup, a recipe he'd never tried, he realised he couldn't delay any longer. Every hour spent with Helmut made his mission more difficult. What he found impossible to stomach was the fact that he actually liked him, could actually see his problems, and understood why he didn't enjoy being organised by an overpowering daughter.

"A go-getter," Helmut had said. She was certainly that. Her supreme self-confidence coloured everything she did. The way she spoke, the way she drove, and the way she dressed. She was a striking woman, with her dark hair swept back off her face, high cheek bones, large brown eyes, and a perfect nose. Only her lips betrayed her. Under the brilliant lipstick they were thin, no fullness, no generosity.

Once the waiter had cleared the soup dishes Josepha relaxed and smiled at Andrew. He felt it was the beginning of campaign.

'You don't know how pleased I am to meet you. A kindred spirit for my father. Someone who has so much in common with him.'

'My English ancestors, maybe?' said Helmut.

'What!'

'I thought, maybe that's why you were following me.'

'Following you!'

'My grandmother was English. Perhaps I resembled your father?

A watery smile crossed Andrew's face. 'No, no you don't.'
Josepha aware of the slight tension crashed in. 'What did you do during the war, Herr Pringle?'

'I was in the RAF.' There, it was out before he'd had time to think. God, why had he mentioned it?

'You were! What a coincidence. Dada was in the Luftwaffe.' Helmut paused halfway through his Fischragout which he found far too much for him. 'You are full of surprises, Andrew. What was your job?'

'A pilot,' said Andrew shortly.

'And what did you fly?'

'Lancasters.'

There was silence, a silence Josepha couldn't understand, covering a strange undercurrent.

Of course, thought Helmut, a faint glimmering of an idea surfacing, of course I've been to England.

The restaurant noises faded. Helmut felt the plane lurch as it was buffeted by force 8 winds which had been predicted. He kept his head and concentrated on keeping his distance from the Lancasters surrounding him. The squadron flew higher into mist and out of the wind. Flying for three hours and expecting at any moment to be discovered was an eerie experience, but he'd better not think about it. He'd been given a job to do. "Destroy them on the ground," the Oberst had ordered, and then had muttered to himself, "It may be your last chance." Morale on the base was at its lowest ebb. They all knew the war was lost...there was no way out. Suddenly there was laughter as the British bombers reached the English coast no longer observing radio silence.

"Home, James, and don't spare the horses," yelled one airman.

"Over Beechers for the last time," said another.
"Ten to one on Mermaid," said a lilting voice.
"That's a bet you'll lose, Taffy."
What were they talking about, these mad English who were unaware of a rogue in their midst?

'Dada, Dada are you all right?' Josepha's voice penetrated the past.

'Yes, yes, day dreaming.'

'You have a guest, father. Perhaps you should let us into the secret?'

'There's no secret, Josepha, but I do find the similarities between Andrew's life and mine remarkable. We've both worked in Local Government, we are both widowers with one daughter, and now to crown it all I find we were both pilots.'

'Well, well,' laughed Joanna, 'this coincidence may solve my problem. I heard this morning, Dada, that I have to leave for Hanover immediately to take over the Head Office PR for at least two weeks because Fritz Beck has had another heart attack.'

'You'll enjoy that.'

'No I won't. You know I can't leave you at home on your own.'

'Of course you can.' Helmut was annoyed. 'I'm quite capable of looking after myself.'

'I have asked Frau Stein to come in every day to keep an eye on you. Do the washing, shopping, and cook your evening meal.'

'Josepha, I don't want Frau Stein in the house. Her constant chatter drives me mad. It is my home, Josepha, and I'll stay there alone.'

'No, you will not father. But...' her eyes lit up as a brilliant idea struck her, 'perhaps Herr Pringle might like to stay with you for a few days? You have so much in common, you'd have plenty to talk about, and it would ease my mind.'

Andrew couldn't believe his good fortune. Fate was playing into his hands. Schmidt might not agree, of course. He was so obviously looking forward to being on his own, two weeks of peace while his bossy daughter organised other people.

'I am sure, Josepha, that Andrew would much rather be independent and remain at the Gasthaus.'

'Oh no,' Andrew found himself saying, 'I'd have no objection to moving in with you for a few days, if that's what you'd like.'

'There, that's settled, ' said Josepha.

'No, it isn't,' said Andrew quietly. 'Your father needs time to think it over. He may prefer to be on his own.'

Helmut had already made up his mind. Test his theories. Find out why the Englishman had been trailing him.'I'd be pleased, Andrew, to welcome you into my home.'

'Good,' said Josepha. 'That's settled then, and after lunch I'll run you back to Bernkastel in the car.'

'But we have return tickets,' protested Helmut.

'It will take you two hours by river, and only fifteen minutes by road. I need to get back home, pick up some clothes, and transfer Herr Pringle's baggage. I must be on my way by 3 o'clock.'

Inspector Julian Venning who'd collected his hired car from the Haus Constanze waited at the quayside for the *Brünhilde* to dock. Passengers speaking many languages streamed across the gangplank, but a tall elderly Englishman was not among them. Damnation! Where the hell is he? Venning ran for his car, drove into the centre of the town and up the hill to St Michaels's Gasthaus. He rang the bell on the counter and waited impatiently for Fräulein Jürgens to appear.

'Ah, Herr Venning, you are too late. Your father paid his bill and left.'

'What!'

'I told him you were looking for him....told him it was an important family matter. He looked surprised, perhaps a little startled too, but all he did was shake his head and smile.'

'When did he leave?'

'Early afternoon, soon after lunch.'

'Where did he go?'

'I'm sorry, sir, but he didn't say. He paid his account, thanked me very much, took his suitcase with him, and left.'

'Did he leave a forwarding address?'

'No, sir.'

'Thank you Fräulein.'

Josepha was in a hurry and exasperated when she noticed a red Porsche had parked in her usual place adjacent to the church. Andrew, sitting in the back seat, had been prepared. Whoever was looking for him, whoever it was who'd lied about an urgent family matter was now sitting in the Porsche waiting. He dropped some coins on the floor of the car and bent down to pick them up. It took an unconscionable time to find them, but by the time he'd located the last pfennig, Josepha had driven into the parking lot opposite the house. As he emerged from the car the Porsche was out of his line of sight.

The Inspector drove slowly up Burgstrasse. There by the church sat the damned Porsche. At least it meant Schmidt was still alive. But for how long? Andrew, a man he didn't know, was far more resourceful, astute and single-minded than he'd imagined. He caught a glimpse of Lieutenant Neal, and the driver but where was the third man? The man with fair curly hair who'd gazed at him as he left the gasthaus that morning? Keeping a watch, perhaps, on the back of the house? Only one way to find out. Park the car and make tracks.

Vines covered the entire hillside behind the church, graveyard and Helmut's garden. It wasn't an easy walk. Running along each small terrace of vines were thick slates which retained the day's heat and gave off enough warmth during the night to protect the grapes. He had to be careful not to bruise the fruit as he moved between the rows. There! There it was again. A movement in the cemetery. A brief glimpse of the top of an Alpine hat with a feather in it. Good God, the man was crouched behind an enormous headstone. What good would that do? Venning made no attempt to hide. He walked upright until he came to Helmut Schmidt's garden. There he could see conifers of all shapes and sizes, a long lawn, and a paved area, shaded by a pergola covered in Russian Lilac. A table and several wooden chairs were visible, but no one sitting there to enjoy the afternoon sun. It was impossible to see the ground floor of the house effectively hidden by Venninges and trees. From the vineyard he went through a gate marked *PRIVATE* into the graveyard.

'You can come out, soldier,' he yelled. 'you'll see nothing on all fours.'

The man red about the gills and puffing slightly stood up. 'You're the policeman, I suppose? he said belligerently.'

'You've got it in one.'

The man from intelligence fished a small walkie-talkie out of his pocket.

'Redbreast, you hearing me?'

'Yes. Carry on sergeant.'

'I've got company. The policeman's just shown up.'

'Let me speak to him.'

The fair haired sergeant thrust the gadget at Venning. 'You play with it, SIR. Press that button.'

'What do you want, Lieutenant?'

'That was a dirty trick you pulled this morning, sir.'

'You mean you'd rather have had decaffeinated?'

'I mean we should be working together. Group made it quite clear that we had to do everything possible to avoid an international incident. He said you needed back-up.'

'I do, Lieutenant, but you've signalled your intentions loud and clear by parking that damned car outside the church.'

'We thought it would act as a deterrent, sir.'

Nothing, thought Venning, will deter him. 'Has there been any movement, Lieutenant?'

'Yes, sir. A woman driving a BMW, maybe his daughter, arrived with Schmidt nearly an hour ago. She's still in the house.'

'Good. Now, lieutenant, this is how I suggest we play it. Leave your man in position behind the house, and get your driver to park the Porsche down by the river and stay with it ___ on call, of course, and I suggest you join me.'

'Where?'

'There's a small VW parked a 100 yards up the road. I'll be with you as soon as I'm able.' Venning handed back the walkie-talkie. 'Sergeant, I want you to stay hidden while I take a look at the house. Lend me your hat,' and without more ado

Operation Giselle © Teresa Collard   174

Venning took it off the head of the astonished sergeant, and threw it into the garden where it lodged among a border of brilliant blue hydrangeas.

'What's that for, sir?'

'It's windy isn't it? If anyone asks why I'm in the garden I'm looking for my hat.'

Shutting the gate behind him Venning stepped down into the garden and made his way to the paved area praying that Schmidt didn't have a pet Doberman ready to pounce. From where he stood the ground floor was still masked by Venninges but through an upstairs window he caught a glimpse of a dark haired woman moving to and fro, bending down, straightening up, and then back to a wardrobe which was open. She's packing, thought Venning. In a hurry too. I wonder whether they're both going away? The Inspector who had a reputation for working intuitively felt that 'D' Day for Andrew had arrived, otherwise why had he left the gasthaus? But where was his luggage? Ready for a quick get-away? But Andrew could be stymied by an unknown factor. If Schmidt was going on holiday it would give him and Dadswell's men time to find Andrew and persuade him to return home.

Venning crept nearer to the house, hiding behind a thickly leafed viburnum. He could see Schmidt moving around downstairs using his stick. Slowly the German crossed towards the French windows, opened both doors wide, and gazed down the garden. Damn! There's no way he's preparing to go on away. The policeman retreated rapidly to the safety of the conifers, and waited for a few seconds before making a move to retrieve the hat. He then quietly unlatched the gate, threw the hat to the fair haired sergeant, told him to keep his head down, and made his way back to the VW.

Lieutenant Neal studied the red-haired, red-bearded man who was walking swiftly towards the car. A man who didn't look like a policeman, who could have been taken for a sea captain; a man who would be immovable in a scrum; a man who pushed his staff to their uttermost, and a man who never spared himself. Venning produced the keys, and the two men climbed into the hired car which felt like a hothouse.

'We'll grow etiolated in this heat and finish up seven foot high and pale as death,' growled the lieutenant.

Venning grinned. 'We might just sweat a little and lose a pound a two.'

They opened the windows and sat comfortably in silence, both men wondering if they could contain the situation.

'A boring job, surveillance,' said the army man. 'We could spend days sitting here.'

'Pleasant enough for the man you've stationed in front of the castle.'

Neal looked smug. 'Corporal Knight needs some suntan.'

As he spoke a BMW eased its way out of the parking lot opposite the house and out into the main road. Lieutenant Neal grabbed his binoculars.

'It's the woman. She's on her own.'

'What a pity,' murmured Venning.

Dinner which Helmut served in the kitchen-diner was a simple meal. A selection of cold meats; salami, garlic sausage, ham, cold frankfurters, and a mixed salad.

'I hope you'll find this meal adequate, Andrew?'

'Yes, yes there's more than enough. I eat less and less these days.'

'That's our age, my friend. We're not young men any longer, burning up calories by playing football, squash, or running marathons.'

'I'm not on the dust heap yet,' said Andrew as he chewed a tough frankfurter. 'I still play tennis.'

'Now, my friend,' said Helmut as he extracted a bottle from the ice-bucket, you must sample my favourite wine from Urzig. First the Kabinett with the meat, and then the Auslese with the chocolate mousse, not home made, I'm, afraid.'

Andrew laughed. 'For widowers, that's par for the course. I fill my freezer once a month with everything I need from bread to bacon which means I don't waste precious time, which can be spent in the garden. Shopping, Helmut, is anathema. My wife insisted on fresh this, and fresh that, even when it wasn't available. I'll swear half my waking hours were spent in supermarkets.'

'Prost,' said Helmut as he raised his glass.

Andrew finished his mousse, sipped his third glass of Auslese and leaned forward nerving himself for the moment he'd been living for..... waiting for... for nearly half a century. Fate he kept telling himself had willed that he should be here, in this house, alone with his victim. Nemesis, at last! A fair and just retribution to be carried out within the hour. He couldn't leave it any longer. Another day with this man would be disastrous. Each minute, each hour weakened his resolve.

'Are you feeling all right, my friend, or are you a little lethargic after an energetic day and too much wine?'

Dammit! I wish he wouldn't keep calling me his friend. Andrew shook his head. 'I'm OK, not at all tired. I'm fine.'

'Good. You go into the study, and we'll have coffee and liqueurs in comfort.'

'Let me help you clear away.'

'No, no. All I have to do is put the dirty crocks in this damned machine my daughter acquired. You go and sit down. I'll wheel the coffee in on the trolley, an invention I couldn't manage without.'

Andrew opened the study door and stood for some moments wondering whether to kill Helmut the moment he entered the room or wait until he was sitting in an easy chair. Damn! He mustn't think of him as Helmut. He must think of him as a pilot, see him dressed in his fur lined leather jacket, at the controls of a Junkers 88 on a death mission. See him as he dived towards the airfield causing mayhem and destroying three planes, giving Pete and his friends no chance. He took the gun out of his pocket. Such a small toy, such a lethal weapon. One shot would be enough. Helmut with his arthritis would find it impossible to raise himself out of the chair. He'd have to sit and listen. He had to be told why.

The house was detached, far enough away from the neighbours for the shot to pass unnoticed, but he'd better be sure. Closing the window made sense. It was a cosy room. A small desk under the window. A bookcase, no more than 3 foot high ran the full length of one wall. On it were choice pieces of Dresden and a monkey band. The conductor's baton was missing, the violinist had lost his bow, and the drummer his left arm. On the wall above the bookcase were small landscapes and faded photographs taken many years ago.

As Helmut pushed the trolley into the room he noticed that the window had been closed, then with some apprehension, Andrew's preoccupation with the photographs. I'm being stupid, he thought, we should have gone into the sitting room?

'Are these photographs of your family, Helmut?'

'Yes. Yes they are.'
'That small boy looks remarkably like you.'
'It is me.'
'So those two young girls are your sisters?'
'Yes.'
'But I thought you said Josepha was your only relation?'
'Did I?' said Helmut vaguely as he concentrated on pouring the coffee.
'Do you manage to see much of your sisters?'
'No. No, I never see them.'
'Why's that? A family feud or do they live miles away?'
'You really are pressing me, my friend. It's a subject best left alone.'
Andrew swung round to find he was looking at a man whose eyes spoke only of pain.
'If you really must know,' said Helmut quietly, 'it's not something I wanted to burden you with ... my mother and two sisters were all killed in Hamburg in 1943.'

Andrew closed his eyes, but closing his eyes couldn't block out the memory of those horrific nights over Hamburg, where the population was incinerated, where people stood for hours in the river until they collapsed from exhaustion. He recalled the shots showing the firestorm which destroyed everything in its path. He tried not to think of a mother and her two young daughters being burnt alive, but the image persisted. His breath came in spasms. He wanted to vomit. 'Oh, no,' he gasped.

His hand was still on the gun. It was warm and should have been cold.

'Sit down, Andrew. Please sit down, my friend. It's history now. You mustn't take it to heart.'

'But I do,' cried Andrew. Those two small girls with so much to live for... your mother too.'

Andrew stumbled out of the room. He had to get away. To escape from Helmut's measured tones, from his calmness, from his sympathy, from his understanding ... it was more than he could stomach.

Helmut shouted after him in vain. Shouted for him to come back, shouted after him telling him not to take it to heart. But Andrew tormented by his own thoughts, his own guilt, and the faces of the two small girls ran down the hill towards the river.

'My God!' said the Lieutenant, handing the binoculars to Venning. 'Take a look, sir. That must be him. How the hell did he get past us, and into the house?'

Venning pushed the binoculars aside. 'You get in there, Lieutenant, see what you can do for Schmidt; call a doctor; call an ambulance; let's hope he's still alive.'

'Right, sir.'

'And contact your man in the town. Tell my father-in...tell him Pringle is heading down into the town and is armed.'

'He'll cope. He's a hundred percent reliable,' said Neal as he leapt out of the car and walked swiftly towards the house trying, at the same time, to raise Sergeant Foster.

The fleeing man knew he had to stop briefly, get his breath back. give his heart which was pumping away like a traction engine, a rest. Should have listened to Chalmers, didn't give the poor sod a chance. He's gone now, can't apologise, and Emily my love, you knew it all. Knew I was cankered, consumed with hate....never thought that he'd suffered....this unsuspecting man who took me into his home...Emily ...such a slender thread saved me...saved him...saved the man who wasn't too interested in life...he'd had his fill...so Emily have I...I'm diseased...rotten, never used my common sense..."Common sense is all I ask for my boys" that's what mother used to say...a message which I never struck home. Andrew still gasping saw the frightened eyes of a child staring at him, and at the same time accusing him. He ran.

At that moment, Foster who should have been sitting in the Porsche, was in the Gents' loo where the constantly running water and the thick concrete walls reduced Lieutenant Neal's incoming call to a meaningless jumbled jargon. *Come in Redbreast, Come in Redbreast,* emerged as a squawk and his efforts to reply, useless. The attendant in charge of the loos looked at the back of the departing man who, in the act of washing his hands, had rushed out without either drying them or tipping him. The Lieutenant had more success in communicating with Sergeant Nightingale who was now sitting amid the gravestones with only the goose feather protruding. But what the hell was Foster doing? What was going on? Foster's orders were to stay put until needed. Damn the man. Now, what was happening? He switched off the machine Switched it off while he stared in amazement at Helmut Schmidt who stood at his front door shouting after Pringle, imploring on him to return.

Tourists and townsfolk alike wondered why the elderly man was in such a haste. His running had a sense of urgency, a matter of life and death. Venning managed to keep him in view, but the crowds and the narrow streets baulked him. In desperation he dumped the car and followed on foot. Slowly the gap between the two men narrowed, and just as Venning was within 50 yards of his quarry, the fleeing man, despite the rapid beat of his heart and extreme headiness miraculously found a second wind and increased his speed as he made for the bridge. Venning went into top gear, but was still yards away as Andrew reached the bridge. Halfway across, breathless, sweating and swaying he stopped and looked into the water.

'Don't do it, Andrew! Don't do it Andrew!' But the exhausted man didn't throw himself off the bridge. He couldn't have thrown himself off the bridge. He was spent. In his hand he held a small object which, as Venning reached him, he dropped into the river, having no strength to throw it further. Both men looked down on the ever increasing eddy which faded as the wash from a passing barge disturbed the water. Unaware of the man at his side Andrew cried out, 'Emily, Emily, forgive me', before collapsing into the arms of his son-in-law.

There's no way out of this, thought the Inspector bitterly, as he gazed at the tear stained face of Andrew Pringle. I'll have to hand him over to the Germans. As he wiped away the tears and sweat, a crowd which had gathered were all asking what had happened. Everyone seemed to have some advice to offer. Like the Tower of Babel, there were many tongues. Suddenly they stopped. There was a brief hush as a Porsche with a great squeal of brakes drew up alongside. Foster jumped out.

'Message from Lieutenant Neal, sir. Both he and Sergeant Nightingale are at Schmidt's place.'

Venning swallowed hard expecting the worst.

'He said I was to drive you and the old man, I mean Mr Pringle, sir, back to the Constanza. The Lieutenant has already contacted a doctor who'll be there when we arrive. He was bloody right, sir, said Pringle would collapse. Ridiculous to run like that at his age. I'll help you get him in the car, sir.'

'Thanks, Sergeant, but I don't see it the Lieutenant's way. We must go straight to the police. They'll have a doctor on call.'

Venning groaned inwardly. How was he ever going to explain to Joyce that he'd arrested her father? Had had to take him in. She'd suffered enough without all this?

'No need for the police, sir? He hasn't done anything, and there'll be a doctor at...'

'What! What are you saying, Sergeant?'

'Schmidt is alive.'

'Alive,' whispered Venning, but how badly hurt?'

'Not a scratch, sir. Don't think he was even threatened. As far as I can make out from a brief word with my boss, he found Schmidt standing at his front door yelling after Pringle to come back.'

'Thank God, Sergeant, thank God.'

TEN

'No.' said the German doctor as he closed his briefcase. 'Herr Pringle has not suffered a heart attack. His blood pressure is slightly above normal, his heart strong, and his general condition, for a man of his age, excellent.'

Venning looked down on the unconscious man whose face, in repose, gave no secrets away. What had triggered off the headlong race from Schmidt's house into the town? And why did he jettison the revolver?

'He'll be round shortly,' said the doctor. 'Tell him to give up jogging, an overrated pastime.'

'Will you need to visit him again?'

'No. Keep him in bed tonight, and he'll enjoy a good breakfast in the morning. He'll see another twenty years if he uses his common sense.'

Andrew, through a thin layer of consciousness, heard the diagnosis, heard the exchange as the doctor left, which was followed shortly afterwards by the sound of another alien voice as Lieutenent Neal entered the room.

'You look all in, sir. Here take this flask, there'll be a tumbler in the bathroom.'

'Whisky, Lieutenant, that's just what the doctor ordered!

Now, there was a voice he recognised. Andrew opened his eyes. Where was he? How did he get here? He wasn't in hospital. And who was the man with the flask? The man who was leaning over him, whose eyes seen through those thick lenses were enormous.

'The patient's coming round, Inspector.'

'That's a relief, ' said Venning, as he swallowed a hefty whisky in one gulp. Slowly with the aid of the stranger the patient sat up.

'Where am I?'

'In the Haus Constanze,' said the man whose face was strangely familiar.

'Good God, Julian, what are you doing here?'

'Keeping an eye on you,' grinned Venning.

'Is Joyce with you?'

'No, but she'll be relieved to hear you're safe and well.'

'But...how did you know where to find me?' His voice trailed away.

'Of course, idiot that I am, I sent Joyce a postcard.' An explanation, thought Venning, which will do for the moment.

'And who is this?' Andrew looked directly at the bespectacled man.

'I'm Jeremy Neal, sir. I was detailed to help Mr Venning locate you.'

'You're a bit far from home, aren't you? The last time I saw you, you were carrying a rucksack.'

'Oh yes, I'm a great walker.'

'And a great liar too, I'll be bound,' murmured Andrew. Jeremy Neal and Venning looked at each other uneasily. Despite wanting to know exactly what had happened they were treading carefully, but the protagonist was sitting up, prepared to do battle.

Helmut Schmidt, who when Foster had returned with the Porsche, persuaded the Lieutenant to take him with them, was sitting in the TV room wondering why the photographs had caused the man who'd been following him such anguish, emotionally and physically? Somewhere in his subconscious an idea, which had been there for some time, began to grow, but wasn't the idea too far fetched? The stuff on which novels were made. He rose, swearing at his immobility as he made his way into the hall. Room 3, the doctor had said. He could manage the stairs. Slowly and painfully he made his way upstairs to the first floor.

Lieutenant Neal decided that no one, not even a man lying in bed, would get away with calling him a liar.

'Colonel Dadswell gave me orders, Mr Pringle, to keep an eye on you. He didn't much care for your private vendetta.' Andrew laughed. 'How on earth did you manage to lose me?' Before the irate Lieutenant could give vent there was a knock at the door and in walked Schmidt.

'Helmut,' gasped Andrew, 'you shouldn't be here.'

'Neither should you, my friend. You're my guest, and should be staying at the Kastelhaus. Don't shake your head. You made Josepha a promise.

Venning nodded to Jeremy Neal indicating the balcony where they sat silent and tense, straining every muscle as they tried to catch each syllable of the conversation between the two men in the bedroom.

'Andrew, come clean. Tell me why you were following me. Did I mean more than the holy grail? Was I the end of the line?'

'Yes,' whispered Andrew,' but when you know the truth you'll hate me for my pretence...for what you imagined to be friendship and love, was in reality enmity and hatred.'

'That's not true, Andrew. You showed compassion for me. You of all people know how arthritis destroys a person, you saw your own wife suffering.'

'I didn't help her enough....'

'Explain why the death of my mother and sisters distressed you.'

'Because,' and the two men on the balcony could barely hear, 'because I could have been responsible. I flew over Hamburg not once or twice... but four times...'

'Don't take it to heart. You're not responsible. You were given an order, and you obeyed.'

'Yes, yes that's true, but I should have thought about it, realised my guilt instead of...'

'Instead of what?'

'Dwelling on the death of my brother, my twin brother.'

Suddenly everything became clear. The vague ideas in Helmut's sub-conscious emerged with great clarity.

'Your brother was a pilot?

'No. A navigator.'

'Not on the same aircraft?'

'No. In the same squadron.'

'And you saw him shot down over Waddington?'

Andrew nodded.

'By a Junkers 88?'

Again he nodded.

'Oh, my friend, how can you ever forgive me?'

It took Helmut, who was in the garden, a long time to reach the phone.

'Hallo,' he said breathing hard.

'You all right, Dada?'

'Yes.

'What have you been doing?'

'Sitting in the garden. You don't usually call at this time of the day. What's the matter, Josepha?'

'It depends on your reaction to my problem.'

'What are you trying to tell me?'

'I should be at home, Dada, telling you face to face. Beck is dead. He died yesterday.'

Helmut said nothing. He knew what was coming.

'I've been offered the top job, Dada, but it means moving to Hanover.'

'You like Hanover, so I can't see the problem.'

'But you'll have to move too. I hate doing this to you, you love Bernkastel so much, but you will find it easier, really you will, Hanover isn't nearly so hilly.'

'Congratulations Josepha. It's the job you wanted, but you'll be on your own. I'm not moving.'

'What! But I can't leave you. What will you do?'

'It's quite simple. I've already planned to spend six months here and six months in England...' Helmut heard her intake of breath. 'I won't be alone.'

'You mean,' said Josepha seeing her inheritance vanishing before her eyes, 'that the Englishman has moved in with you?'

'Yes. He's been here nearly two weeks, and in that time my arthritis has eased, because I don't have to struggle into town. Andrew does the shopping, and the cooking. He's a good cook; he drives me to Wittlich where we watch a lot of sport; he's fixed the low gear on the motor mower which means I can now mow the lawn myself; he takes me to places I haven't seen for years. You have no worries, Josepha, no worries at all. We're good company. Good for each other.'

Josepha quietly replaced the phone.